STORIES OF
THE ANCIENT GREEKS

THE GODS OF GREECE

STORIES OF
THE ANCIENT GREEKS

BY

CHARLES D. SHAW

illustrated by

GEORGE A. HARKER

YESTERDAY'S CLASSICS

CHAPEL HILL, NORTH CAROLINA

ISBN-10: 1-59915-269-X

ISBN-13: 978-1-59915-269-1

Yesterday's Classics, LLC
PO Box 3418
Chapel Hill, NC 27515

PREFACE

THE tales in this book are old; some of them, it may be, are even older than we suppose. But there is always a new generation to whom the ancient stories must be told; and the author has spent pleasant hours in trying to retell some of them for the boys and girls of to-day.

He remembers what joy it was to him to read about the Greek gods and heroes; and he knows that life has been brighter to him ever since because of the knowledge thus gained and the fancies thus kindled. It is his hope to brighten, if possible, other young lives by repeating for them the immortal fictions and the deathless histories which have been delivered to new audiences for thousands of years.

He feels that he has received valuable help from the keen insight and fine taste of Mr. George A. Harker, whose original drawings adorn and illuminate the volume. The spirit of the book speaks in those animated pictures where action and feeling are so clearly shown.

These stories belong to no one individual; they are the heritage of the race. To help the children of the present time to enter upon this priceless heritage is the aim and desire of

—THE AUTHOR

INTRODUCTION

THE PEOPLE OF OLD GREECE

GREECE is a country of clear blue skies, of sunlit, dancing seas, of tall mountains tipped with snow. At no place within its borders can you be more than forty miles from the sea or ten miles from the mountains.

The rivers hurry down the hill-sides, and no boat sails on their swift current. The winters are very cold, the summers are scorching hot. In the spring the land is beautiful with flowers; in the fall it is rich with ripened fruit and grain. Near the sea-coast grow grapes, olives, figs, oranges, and melons. Farther up among the hills barley and wheat and oak trees are found; higher yet are pine trees and beech trees, and still higher is the line where snow does not melt even in summer.

Eastward from Greece, the sea is full of islands, some large, others small. They also were settled by the Greeks. In the old days each of these was a kingdom by itself. Some were the homes of pirates who lived by robbing the vessels which came and went upon the sea. In others lived the merchants whose ships these pirates robbed.

As the Greeks increased in numbers they sailed from island to island, and reached the coast of Asia Minor. There they built cities which afterwards became rich and famous.

Westward an open sea lies between Greece and Italy. Colonies crossed that water, and settled on the shores beyond the sea. South of Italy lies the large island of Sicily, which also became the home of Greeks who built the famous city of Syracuse.

The first people who made their homes in Greece were called Pelasgians. We know very little about them, except that they must have come from Asia, for in the center of that continent was the earliest home of men. When that region became too crowded the young and strong journeyed east, west, north, and south, looking for new places in which to settle.

At some time, we do not know when, but long before history began to be written, a wandering tribe entered Greece. We cannot tell whether they arrived by sea or land, but very likely it was by sea. They found fertile soil, large forests, and mountains in which were copper, silver, and iron. It is said that they already knew how to farm and that they built cities.

Soon there was the old trouble—not room enough. The young people hitched their oxen to carts, in which they put their few bits of furniture, their children, and the weaker wives, and moved on to find new homes. This happened many times until Greece was dotted all over with small villages.

The rest of the world was also in motion. Other tribes came into this country of Greece and made themselves masters of its farms and towns. The people who had once been the free owners of the land now became slaves, and had to work without pay for others.

Long afterwards the country was called Hellas, and the people were known as Hellenes.

The mountain ranges in Greece run, some north and south, others east and west, so that there are many little valleys, shut away from each other by the high hills.

These valleys were settled by different tribes, among whom there was often war, though they were related to one another and spoke the same language. Those who had homes among the mountains lived by hunting, and on the milk and flesh of their sheep and goats. Those who found more fertile plains became farmers, and raised grain and fruit. Those who lived near the sea became fishermen and sailors.

So they lived for many hundreds of years before any history was written or read. All that time war was going on, cities were building, states were being founded, little vessels were sailing on the narrow seas from island to mainland, men were gradually learning the arts of civilization.

In those dim times cities were begun which afterwards became famous. Three of these were most important, Sparta, Athens, and Thebes. Sparta was the capital of a little district called Laconia or Lacedæmonia.

Athens was the chief city of Attica, and Thebes was the capital of Bœotia.

Sparta had no walls. Every citizen was a soldier, and stood ready to fight for his country night or day.

The people of Thebes and its neighborhood were considered dull and stupid by those who lived in other states.

Athens became the most splendid city in Greece. Her citizens loved everything beautiful. Year after year they built temples and monuments, carved statues, painted pictures, studied poetry, music, and the art of public speaking, and delighted in learning something new.

In the heart of Greece, deep among the mountains, lay the beautiful valley of Arcadia. The people were hunters and shepherds; simple, even rude in their manners, but happy in watching their flocks, and in dancing at their village festivals. They worshiped the god Pan, but beat his image if they had bad luck in hunting.

Some of the Greeks were fierce fighters, others were deep thinkers. For two hundred and fifty years the history of their little country is the history of the world. Their stories have gone into the literature of all Western nations, and nobody can claim to be well-educated who does not know something of them.

This little book is written that children may learn a few of the fables and some of the facts which are part of the treasure of the world. The facts are given as they are told by Herodotus, Thucydides, Xenophon, and Plutarch. No doubt in the course of years fancy has mingled with fact so that the clear truth is hard to find.

It is hoped that this little volume may serve as an introduction to further study for those who have the opportunity, and that the recollection of its contents may give life-long pleasure to such as do not pursue their studies beyond the grammar grade.

NOTE.—In this book will be found many proper names which are strange to young readers. A list of such names, with their pronunciation has been placed at the end of the volume.

CONTENTS

PART I

MYTHOLOGICAL STORIES

PART II

HISTORICAL STORIES

PART I
MYTHOLOGICAL STORIES

CHAPTER I

THE GODS OF GREECE

THE Greeks believed that the world was round and flat. Its outer border was the great river, Ocean. The Mediterranean Sea was in the center of this circle.

Far to the North lived the Hyperboreans in a beautiful land where cold winds did not blow and snow never fell. These people were not obliged to work, and they had no enemies with whom to fight. Sickness and old age did not trouble them. Their lives were happy and tranquil.

In the distant South were the Æthiopians, who were so good and happy that the gods often went to visit them.

In the far-off West were the Fortunate Isles, or "Islands of the Blessed," where everything was charming, and where a few people, beloved by the gods, lived for ever without pain or sorrow.

The Greeks thought there were many gods, most of whom lived above the clouds on top of Olympus, a mountain in Thessaly. They had bodies like men and

1

women, but they were larger, stronger, and usually handsomer than human beings.

The king of all the gods, and the father of many of them, was called Zeus. The Latin name for this god is Jupiter. He was the ruler of the weather. At his command the clouds gathered, rain or snow fell, gentle winds blew, or storms roared. He darted lightning across the sky and hurled thunderbolts upon the world.

The tallest trees and highest mountain peaks were sacred to him.

He was also the god of justice, and sent his servants, the Furies, to punish men and women who did wrong.

His wife was Hera, who in Latin is called Juno. She was very handsome and stately. Her eyes were large and dark, so that one poet called her "ox-eyed." She was proud and quarrelsome and ready to harm those who made her angry.

This couple had several children. One of them, Hephæstus, the Latin Vulcanus, is said by some to have been born lame. Others say that his father in a fit of anger threw him out of heaven. He fell for a long summer day, and when he reached the island of Lemnos he had little life remaining in him, and limped forever after. He was the blacksmith god, who built houses for the other gods and made the scepter of Zeus, the arrows used by Apollo and Artemis, and other wonderful things. He was good-natured and fond of fun, but not foolish. Volcanoes were called his earthly workshops.

His wife was Aphrodite, the Latin Venus, the loveliest of all the goddesses, who was said to have been born from the foam of the sea. She was the ruler of love and beauty. Wherever she went soft and gentle breezes followed her, and flowers sprang up where her feet touched. She made some people happy, but for others she caused much grief and trouble.

One day Zeus had a terrible headache. Hephæstus, with an ax, split open his father's aching head. The goddess Athene, the Latin Minerva, sprang out, full grown and dressed in armor. She became the goddess of wisdom, and also took care of cities. She never married but lived alone in her house upon Mount Olympus.

Phœbus, the Latin Apollo, was the god who ruled the sun. He loved music and poetry.

Artemis, the Latin Diana, was his twin sister. She had charge of the moon and was the friend of the hunters.

Hermes, the Latin Mercurius, whence our Mercury, was handsome and swift, the messenger of the gods. Under his care were merchants, travelers, and public speakers. He wore a low-crowned hat with wings, and wings grew from his ankles. In his hand, he carried a wand around which snakes twined. He was very cunning and full of tricks.

Ares, the Latin Mars, was the god of war, finding pleasure in battle and death.

Hestia, the Latin Vesta, was the sister of Zeus. She was the goddess of the fireside and watched over the homes of men. She never married, but Zeus gave her a seat in the center of his palace and sent her the sweetest morsels at every feast. On earth she was worshiped as the oldest and best of the gods. In her temple a sacred fire was kept forever burning, watched by unmarried women, who were called "Vestal Virgins."

These ten gods formed the "Great Council" of Olympus. They lived in their own houses of brass, built by Hephæstus, but every day they went to the palace of Zeus and feasted on ambrosia and nectar. Hebe, the beautiful daughter of Zeus and Hera, waited upon the table. After her marriage to Heracles her place was taken by Ganymede, a beautiful Trojan boy, whom Zeus in the form of an eagle carried away to heaven. At the feasts Apollo played on his lyre and the Muses sang. The Muses were nine sisters, who lived on Mount Parnassus. They had charge of poetry, history, music, tragedy, comedy, dancing, love-songs, hymns, and astronomy.

The ruler of the sea was Poseidon, whose Latin name was Neptune. Under the waves he had a shining palace, the work of Hephæstus.

Demeter, the Latin Ceres, was goddess of the earth, especially of harvests of grain. Dionysus, or Bacchus, was the god of vineyards and wine, and was particularly adored by the Greeks. Eros, the Latin Cupid, the little god of love, was the son of Venus. Eos was the goddess of the dawn. Iris was the messenger of Hera, and the road by which she traveled from heaven to earth was the rainbow, which vanished when her errand was done.

There were three Fates, who spun the thread of human life and cut it off at their pleasure.

There were three Graces, who favored everything beautiful and charming in manners and dress.

There were also three Furies, who had snakes for hair and were frightful to look at. It was their duty to follow wicked men and women and punish them with dreadful whips.

Nemesis, like the Furies, pursued those who had done wrong, particularly those who had insulted the gods. Wherever she went trouble and sorrow followed.

Momus was the god of laughter, Morpheus of sleep, and Plutus of riches. Plutus was blind and could not see those to whom he gave his gifts. When he approached men he limped slowly along. When he left them he flew away.

All these went and came as they pleased, being sometimes in the sky, sometimes on the earth. They did not always do right, and they often quarreled and fought among themselves. Although they could not be killed, they could be wounded. Then *ichor* instead of blood flowed from their veins. They took much interest in human affairs; they had their favorites whom they helped, and their enemies whom they tried to harm.

CHAPTER II

FIRE FROM HEAVEN

T HE Greeks believed that this earth, on which we live, was once a great heap of matter, in which land and water and air were all mixed together. There was no light or life anywhere except among the gods in heaven.

After a while the gods agreed to put this heap into shape and order. They separated the air from the earth and water. The air being lightest flew up, and formed the sky. The earth being heavy sank down, but the water flowed all around it and held it up, so that it should not sink entirely away.

Then the gods gave form to the earth. They lifted up the mountains, and that left valleys. They dug paths for the rivers; they set islands in the sea, they made the world look as it now does.

They also fashioned the sun and moon and stars, and these gave light. The mountains were soon covered with young trees; grass and flowers grew on the plains; fish were in the sea, birds flew in the air, and animals moved about on the dry land.

All these living creatures were made by two lower gods called Titans. Their names were Prometheus and Epimetheus. They also created man, nobler than the animals, because he walks upright and looks toward heaven, while the other creatures walk on four feet and look downward to the ground.

Epimetheus did the work, and Prometheus was the overseer. The animals had different gifts. The ox was very strong, the horse could run fast, the owl was wise, the fox was cunning, the eagle had wings, lions and bears had teeth and claws to fight with, the snake had poison to kill its victims or its enemies.

Birds had feathers, and beasts had fur, or wool, or hair, to keep them warm. Even oysters and clams had little houses of shell in which they could shut themselves up tight. But man had no feathers, or fur, or wool, or shell, and not a great deal of hair. When his turn came to receive some special gift there was nothing for him. Though he was noblest of all creatures he was really weakest and most helpless of all.

The two Titan brothers stood and looked at each other. "What shall we do now?" said Epimetheus. "Everything has been given out."

"Is nothing left?" said Prometheus.

"Nothing at all," answered his brother.

They looked all around, but no help came. Then they looked up at the shining sun.

"Oh, I know!" said Prometheus. "Stay here and wait for me."

"Where are you going?" asked his brother.

"You will know when I come back," answered Prometheus.

Then he went to the highest mountain and climbed to its top. There Athene, the goddess of wisdom, met him and helped him the rest of the way up to the sky. On the mountain top he had broken a branch from a pine tree. This he took with him, and as the sun came driving by in his chariot of fire, Prometheus touched the branch to the burning wheels. The green leaves snapped and crackled in the flame, the pitchy wood took fire. Prometheus hurried back from the sky and ran down the mountain. All the way he took care to keep the branch burning.

When he reached Epimetheus, he said, "Hurry and get a pile of branches. Here is a fire from heaven. This shall be our one best gift to man. By this he shall conquer all the other creatures and be master of earth and sea and air."

Epimetheus ran and gathered branches and piled them in a heap. Prometheus threw his torch among them. The twigs caught fire at once, and soon there was a bright, roaring cheerful, comfortable blaze. Then the brothers called the man and said, "Come here and be warm;" for the night was falling, and the air was growing chilly. The man stretched out his hands toward the fire and laughed. "This is not a plaything," said the Titans, "You must keep it as your servant, and be very careful that you never let it become your master. Use

FIRE FROM HEAVEN

it rightly, and it will make you ruler over everything in the world."

So the man was glad, and kept the fire burning. When the winter came he did not have to travel south, like the birds, or go to sleep in a hollow tree, like the bears. He made a fire in his hut, and was comfortable there. Soon he learned to cook his food instead of eating it raw. He found stones which would melt, and which we call ores,—lead ore, tin ore, zinc ore, copper ore, gold ore, silver ore. He melted gold and silver, and with stone hammers pounded out rings and bracelets and earrings, which he wore. He melted copper and zinc together and made bronze. This he hammered into spear heads, which he fastened on long sticks. Then he could fight the lion and the bear, keeping out of reach of their claws. With these spears he could also catch fish. Afterwards he made bronze hooks for fishing. He learned the use of the bow, and tipped his arrows with bronze. So he could shoot flying birds, or running deer, or crawling snakes. He made bronze bits for horses, and axes for cutting down trees, and plowshares for tilling the ground. Thus he had much better tools of every kind than the stones he used at first.

Long afterwards men found out how to melt and shape iron, which was better and more useful than bronze. So the fire from heaven gave men mastery over every animal, and made them rulers of the earth.

CHAPTER III

THE MAGIC BOX

S O far, man lived alone upon the earth. He gathered some animals about him,—the horse to ride, the ox for the plow, the dog for friendship. But none of these could talk to him. They had voices and made noises, but they could not speak as he could. He was lonely in his wide and beautiful world.

Zeus, the father of the gods, called his family together. "Look down to earth," he said. "Do you see that creature walking upright there?"

They answered, "Yes, great Father! We see him."

"He is lonely," said Zeus. "Let us give him a companion. He is man. I will form a woman to be with him, and each of you shall give her something that shall be a part of her life."

The gods and goddesses were pleased. Zeus created the woman, but she had yet no life. Aphrodite bent down and kissed her on cheeks and lips. A lovely flush appeared on her face, her mouth became rosy and smiling, she had received the gift of beauty.

Athene drew near, and gently laid her hand

upon the woman's brow. "My gift is wisdom," she said. "This woman shall be wise to spin, to weave, to do all manner of household work, and to train up children in goodness."

The shining god Apollo came up, and touched her lips and her fingers.

"I give her the power of music," he declared. "She shall be able to sing sweet songs of love and home and hope and heaven. From reeds and strings she shall be able to draw pleasant sounds to cheer man when he is tired, and to comfort him when he is sad."

Then Ares, the god of war, looked at her and said, "She will not be a fighter herself, but she shall be the cause of many wars. That is my gift. I have no other."

Hephæstus, the blacksmith, limped up and said, "I will put iron in her blood. That will make her strong to bear trouble and endure hardship. Smaller and finer than man, she shall be more patient and steadfast than he."

Eros brought for his gift a warm and tender heart. "She is lovely and shall be loving," he said.

Last of all came Hermes, the swift-running god. His eyes twinkled as he touched her ears, her eyes and her nose.

"My gift is curiosity. To see everything, to hear everything, and to know everything, that shall be her wish," he said. Then he touched her tongue, but did not say anything more.

Zeus stretched forth his golden scepter, and laid it lightly upon her head.

"Arise, woman!" he exclaimed. She arose and stood upon her feet.

"The gods have given you their gifts," he declared.

"Your name shall be Pandora," which means "All-gifts."

"Hermes," he called, "take this woman down to earth and give her to man, to be his companion for better and for worse, for sorrow and for joy. Take with you also this box, her wedding present, which must never be opened. Go, perform your duty."

Hermes took Pandora by the hand, and soon they were on the earth. They entered the man's hut, and Hermes said, "This is your wife, sent you by Zeus. Her name is Pandora. Here is your wedding present, this box which must never be opened. Farewell."

The man was very happy with his new companion. She was beautiful, kind, gentle, and cheerful. He showed her his knives and hammers, axes and saws, his bow and spear, arrows and fishhooks, his plow and hoe, and everything that he had made of bronze. She told him how to make a distaff and spindle for spinning, and how to build a loom for weaving. She asked him to make hairpins for her hair, and needles to sew with, and knitting needles that she might knit stockings and caps.

When the man went out to work she stayed in the

house. In one corner of the room stood the magic box, her wedding present. If she was spinning or weaving, or sewing or knitting, she was always looking at that. It was of ivory, beautifully carved.

She often said, "I do wonder what it holds. It is so handsome outside that the inside must be very lovely."

Sometimes she laid down her work and went to the box. She looked at it with her eyes, listened at it with her ears, sniffed at it with her nose. But she could never be sure that there was any sound or any odor. She began to be worried. The gift of Hermes was giving her a great deal of trouble.

Often at night she would wake up and say to her husband, "I do wonder what is in the box."

He would answer, "It is not to be opened. Go to sleep. I am tired."

But she could not rest day or night. Always she wondered what was in that strange box. Why was it given if it must never be opened?

At last she could bear it no longer. She lifted the lid just a little. There was a stir and rush in the box, the lid was thrown wide open, and out flew a multitude of things with wings. They seemed like wasps and hornets and stinging insects, but they were worse. They were trouble, sorrow, sickness, distress, pain, anger, envy, hatred, malice, falsehood, everything ugly and dreadful.

Pandora clapped down the lid, too late. These

PANDORA AND HER BOX

creatures buzzed in her ears, settled in her hair, filled the hut, and flew out of the window over all the world.

Pandora sank down, crying as if her heart would break. Then she heard a knocking in the box, and a little voice saying, "Let me out."

She raised the lid, and a charming little creature came out of the box.

"Poor Pandora!" she said. "My name is Hope. I will stay with you and comfort you. You can never get rid of the trouble you have caused by opening the box, but I was sent to cheer you and to help you bear your trials."

That was all the good that Pandora got from the magic box. When everything else was against her she still had hope.

CHAPTER IV

THE VOICES OF THE GODS

W HEN the people wished to know the will of the gods they inquired at places called "oracles." The most famous of these was at Delphi. There was an opening in the ground, out of which came a strange gas or vapor. Over this place a temple was built and dedicated to Apollo. A priestess lived there, and when people desired to have their fortune told she breathed the vapor, and what she said afterwards was thought to be the answer of the god. But it was hard to understand, and the priests had to explain it to the visitors. Usually it could be taken in two or three ways, so that, whatever happened, the oracle would be right.

Once the people of Athens asked what they should do in a time of great danger. The oracle told them to trust to their wooden walls. Some hurried to the ships and escaped, but others trusted in the wooden walls on the Acropolis, the citadel of Athens, and fought bravely there, only to be defeated.

This is the way in which the oracle at Delphi was discovered. Some goatherds, feeding their flocks on

Mount Parnassus, found that when the animals ate near a certain place they seemed to go crazy, and ran about bleating until they fell down in a fit. The men, looking for the cause of this, found a long, deep crack in the side of the mountain. One of them bending over and looking down breathed the vapor which came from the opening. He threw up his arms, ran among his fellow-herdsmen with a wild look on his face, and shouted out strange words which no one understood. Then he fell down weak and trembling, and could not rise for some time. His friends were frightened, and, since they could not explain the matter, they thought it must be the breath of some god that had driven him wild. It was decided at last that this god must be Apollo. A temple was built, and a priestess, called the Pythoness, was appointed. She washed at the fountain of Castalia, put a laurel wreath on her head, and sat on a tripod, or three-footed chair, near the opening. Visitors asked their questions, and she answered in the name of the god.

There was an oracle of Zeus at Dodona. It is said that two black doves flew from Egypt into Greece. One alighted on an oak tree in Dodona, and said to the people, "Here shall be the oracle of the mighty Zeus. You who would know the will of the father of the gods and men come here and listen. He will speak and you shall learn."

The other dove flew to the Libyan oasis, and alighted on the roof of the temple of Jupiter, speaking the same words to the people there. After that, in both these places, the leaves of the trees whispered, and the priests explained what they said.

The oracle of Trophonius was in Bœotia. He and his brother were architects, and built a treasure-house for a king. They set a stone in one of the walls in such a way that they could move it whenever they liked, and so go in and take the money and jewels without exciting suspicion. The king was astonished to find his treasure disappearing, though all the locks were fast and the seals unbroken. He set a trap in the treasury, and the brother was caught. Trophonius could not get him out, so he cut off his brother's head and took it with him, going out by way of the secret stone. Soon after the earth opened and swallowed up the "Master-Thief," as he has been called.

A great drought fell on Bœotia, and the people went to Delphi for help. They were told to consult the oracle of Trophonius at Lebadea. No oracle was found there until one man noticed a swarm of bees flying into an opening in the ground. Following them he heard a voice that told him what he wished to know.

Those who visited that oracle had to go down a narrow passage into a cave, and only by night. Coming out they must walk backward. They were always low-spirited after such a visit, so that when any one was sad and gloomy, people said, "He must have been to the oracle of Trophonius."

CHAPTER V

DEUCALION'S FLOOD

THE Greek poets say that the first men lived in happiness and innocence for many years. That was the Golden Age. After it came the Silver Age, when men were not quite so happy or so good. The Brazen Age followed, with everything growing worse and worse. Then came the Iron Age, and wickedness and wrong were everywhere. Nobody was happy; love was dead; cruelty, murder, robbery, and war filled the whole world.

Zeus, king of heaven, called a meeting of the gods. They went to his palace, and he told them of the wickedness of mankind.

"The sins of men rise up like a black cloud," he said. "There are no songs of praise, only cries of the unhappy. No smoke of sacrifice ascends, but the smell of burning homes comes up and spreads itself through heaven. Men hate one another and do not love the gods. I will destroy this wicked race, and bring a better people upon the earth."

At first he thought he would send lightning and

burn up all; then he considered that water might serve him better. He sent out the stormy winds, and the sky grew black with heavy clouds from which rain poured down. He called on his brother Poseidon to unchain the ocean, and soon its waters rolled high over the shores. The rivers rose, the ground rocked with earthquakes. Temples and houses fell, valleys filled with water, beasts and men were swept away. Villages vanished, cities were seen no more; only the mountains appeared, and on their tops and sides animals and human beings were gathered trembling. The wolf stood by the lamb but did not harm it; the lion crowded close against the deer, and both were alike afraid. Men did not strike each other; they lifted up their hands in prayer to the gods. Women did not look into mirrors; they looked to heaven for pity and help.

The waters rose higher. The animals were gone, so were all the men who did not have boats. The waves were high and fierce. They dashed the boats against the rocks, and they sank.

Only one mountain stood out of the water. That was Parnassus. Only one boat floated on the sea, and in it were a man and his wife, Deucalion and Pyrrha. They had been good when everybody else was bad, and Zeus had taken care of them through the storm and the flood.

The winds fell, the rain stopped, the boat rested on the mountain side. Ocean drew back his waves, the valleys were filled with roaring rivers that carried away the water to the sea. Deucalion and Pyrrha stepped out of the boat and stood upon the ground.

"O, wife," the good man said, "I am afraid we are alone in the world! All our friends and neighbors are gone. There is nobody to help us, or tell us what to do! No! I am wrong in saying that. There are yet the gods and we will ask their advice."

They went down the mountain a little way to a place where they knew there had been an oracle. The cave was there, but no altar burned, and no priest stood near.

They went into the cave and knelt down. "O goddess!" they said, "thou dwellest in the dark, yet seest all things. Behold two sorrowful creatures who are left alone in a drowned world! We have nothing, we know nothing. We pray to thee, O goddess! Tell us what we ought to do."

A strange, solemn voice answered, "Cover your heads. Loosen your girdles. Go down the mountain, and, as you go down cast your mother's bones behind you."

They were frightened and did not understand. How could they find their mother's bones when everything had been swept away in the dreadful flood? They were no wiser than they had been, until Deucalion thought, "Why, the earth is our great mother, to be sure. Her bones,—why, those must be the stones. Let us see if that is what the oracle means."

They covered their heads and loosened their

belts, and went down the mountain. As they went they stooped and picked up stones and threw them back over their shoulders. Presently they heard a sound of running feet and of voices. They looked back. Young men were following Deucalion, holding out their hands to him and calling him "Bab-ba!" Young girls were running hard after Pyrrha, trying to catch her dress, and murmuring "Mam-ma!"

Deucalion threw another stone, and watched to see what would happen. Another young man started up to run and call. Pyrrha threw again, and a new young woman joined the company of girls.

The old people went down into the valley, and by the time they reached it they had a large family of grown-up children, whom they taught to build houses, to plow the ground, to plant vines, to weave and sew, and to talk the Greek language. So the world was peopled again, and all the Greeks look back to Deucalion and his wife as their great ancestors.

CHAPTER VI

IN THE WOODS

AMONG the Greeks every trade or business was believed to be under the care of some god or goddess. The god of shepherds was called Pan. He lived in caves and forests, and was fond of dancing with the satyrs and Dryads. He invented the shepherd's pipe of reeds, with which he made sweet music.

Satyrs were creatures who lived in the woods. They were neither man nor beast, but looked like both. Their heads and bodies were human, but were covered with short hair. They had feet like those of goats, and on their heads grew two short horns.

Dryads, or Hamadryads, were the beings who lived in the trees. Each had a tree which was her home and of which she was the life. She could come out and dance and play for a while, but if she stayed away for too long her tree withered and perished. When a tree was cut down or died, its Dryad died with it. This belief made the people careful not to hurt trees without good cause.

Groves, or clumps of trees, were often sacred

to the gods. There was one very large oak dedicated to Demeter. It measured nearly twenty-five feet around the trunk, and it was higher than any of the trees among which it stood.

The man who owned the grove wished to build a boat. He said to his servants, "That oak is just what I need; get axes and cut it down."

One of them answered, "Master, we do not like to do that. It is sacred to the goddess, and she will not be pleased."

"Goddess!" he cried, "what is the goddess to me? Do I not own the tree? Is it not my right to cut it down? Say no more, but strike."

They did not move. He took an ax and angrily struck the tree. The thick trunk shivered and seemed to groan. Blood flowed from the cut made by the ax. Those who stood by were frightened, and one of them took hold of his master's arm and begged him not to strike again.

"See, master," he said, "see the blood! You heard that dreadful groan. You are killing the Dryad as well as the oak."

"Slave," shouted the master, "do you dare to touch me? Though it were the goddess herself I would cut it down. But you shall be rewarded for your piety. Take that, good man!"

He struck the servant a heavy blow with the ax.

Then the tree spoke. A solemn voice said, "I have long lived in this tree as its guardian spirit. Demeter

THE TREE KILLER

knows me and loves me. I die, and your hands kill me. Wicked enemy of the gods, you shall be punished. Remember my dying words!"

The man forced his slaves to cut down the tree. In its fall it broke down many of its neighbors, and the beauty of the grove was gone forever.

The Dryads who lived there went in a sad procession to Demeter.

"Mother!" they said, "behold our mourning garments and pity our tears. A wicked man has killed our sister and destroyed your holy grove. O mother, punish him as he deserves!"

The goddess nodded her head. She thought of a dreadful punishment for the cruel and wicked man. She would give him into the power of Famine.

She called an Oread, or mountain spirit.

"You must carry a message for me," she said. "Far away in the icy land of Scythia is a place where there are no trees and no crops. Cold and Fear and Famine live there. It has been ordered that Famine and I can never come together, but tell her from me that she must go to that wicked tree killer and enter into him and make him entirely her own. Take my chariot and go quickly!"

The Oread mounted the chariot, and after a long drive came to the field of Famine. It had no grain, or grass, or trees,—only rocks. Famine was digging with her nails in the ground. Her face was pale, her lips were white, her eyes were sunken, the flesh was drawn tight over her bones. Even the Oread could not go very near her.

So she called out what Demeter had told her to say, and drove away as fast as possible, for the very sight of Famine had made her hungry.

Famine went by night to the room of the tree killer. He was asleep. She folded him in her wings and breathed her spirit into him, then flew away.

He woke up in the middle of the night, very hungry. His family gave him food, but could never give him enough. He ate all the time, yet always grew more hungry.

He sold his property piece by piece and bought food. At last everything was gone, and he was as hungry as ever.

Then he took his daughter to the slave market by the sea and sold her. She prayed to Poseidon. "O kind god of the sea!" she said, "do not let a poor, innocent girl be sold into slavery. Save me from this dreadful fate!"

The sea-god answered her prayer. In a moment she seemed no longer a girl, but a fisherman busy with his net. The man who had bought her was surprised not to see his new slave.

"Fisherman," he said, "have you seen a poorly dressed girl who had her hair down over her shoulders, and who was crying? It is only an instant since she stood where you are and now she seems to be gone."

The girl was delighted that he did not know her. She answered, "Good stranger, you see that I am very busy with my net. But I tell you truly that for the last half hour I have seen nobody on this spot except myself."

The owner went off, thinking that his slave had run away. Then Poseidon changed her back to her own self. Her father sold her again many times, but the god always changed her before she could be taken away. Sometimes the buyer saw a horse, or a bird, or a cow or a deer, but never the girl. Still her father could not get enough food. He began to eat himself, and that was the last of him. So the tree killer, Erysichthon, was punished.

A young man named Rhœcus, walking in a forest, saw an oak tree ready to fall to the earth. The wind had loosened its hold on the ground. He put a prop against the tree to keep it upright, and carefully trampled soil around the roots. Suddenly a beautiful creature stood before him. "I am the Dryad of this tree," she said. "You have saved my life. What shall I give to you?"

The young man answered, "Give me your love!"

The Dryad said, "I would do that gladly, but you would soon forget me."

"No," he cried. "That is impossible."

"Very well," she replied. "Come to me here in the wood an hour before sunset. I will send a bee to let you know when it is time."

The young man went away proud and happy. To while away the time he began to play dice with some gay companions. The afternoon passed quickly. A bee flew in at the window and buzzed about his ears. He brushed it away. It came back again and again. He struck at it in anger. The bee darted out of the window. The young man looking after it saw the sunset light just fading from the mountain peak. Too late, he remembered. He hurried to the forest, but all was dark and still. He had lost the Dryad and her love.

CHAPTER VII

UNDER THE WAVES

POSEIDON was the god that ruled the sea. Hephæstus built him a fine house of brass under the water. He did not like to live there alone, so he set out to find a wife.

As the woods were full of tree spirits, so the sea was full of water spirits, who were called Nereids. One of the most beautiful of these was named Amphitrite. She lived with her father and mother in a grotto under the waves. Their home was charming with coral and seashells, and a pretty garden of seaweeds was before the door.

Poseidon had heard of this lovely creature, so he called a dolphin, upon whose back he mounted and rode off to make a visit. He found the nymph very pleasant and agreeable, and she asked him to call again. After a few visits he asked her father if she might be his wife.

The father was entirely willing. When they asked Amphitrite, she said "The mighty ruler of the seas does me too much honor, but I will gladly take him for my husband."

Poseidon was greatly pleased. He said to his dolphin, "Good fish, you must carry double to-day. My bride goes home with me this afternoon, and you shall have a shining reward."

They arrived in safety, and Poseidon said, "Now, faithful dolphin, live no more under the waters, but shine in the sky among the stars."

The happy couple under the sea had a son, called Triton. He went before his father, blowing a trumpet, whenever the king of the sea rode out.

Poseidon did not ride on dolphins any more. He created horses, and harnessed four of them to his chariot. These had hoofs of brass and manes of gold. When the king was going out to drive, Triton blew his horn. The waters became as smooth as glass. Triton went before, the prancing horses drew the chariot, and whales and other huge dwellers in the deep followed after.

Poseidon had another son, called Proteus, who was very wise, and could foretell the future. He could change himself into any shape, and be a seal, a whale, a fish or a man, at his pleasure.

Thetis was another Nereid, and sister of Amphitrite. She married a man, Peleus, and their son was the great Achilles, of whom we shall learn more when we read of the Trojan war.

An insane husband once chased his wife who was

carrying their little boy. Coming to the edge of a cliff which overhung the sea, in her fright she leaped into the water. The gods who were sorry for her, changed her into a sea-goddess, called Leucothea, and her son into a god named Palæmon. He generally rode upon a dolphin. Sailors in danger of shipwreck prayed to him and his mother, and they often answered such prayers, for they remembered how kind the gods had been to them.

Every river and every fountain had guardian spirits. These were called Naiads, and are shown in pictures as beautiful young women.

They were generally friendly to mankind, but sometimes they carried their favorites away from home and family. So they did with Hylas. He was a very good-looking lad, who, being in a strange country, went to a spring for water.

One of the Naiads saw him, and called to the others, "Oh, come, see this pretty boy!"

He bent down to fill his pitcher, but saw sweet faces jumping up out of the water.

"Oh, pretty boy!" they said. "Do you live near here? We never before saw you at this spring."

Hylas blushed and said, "No, I am a stranger, and must hurry back to the ship and my friends."

"Oh, no!" they said. "Do not go away. Stay with us!"

They stretched up their arms out of the water, caught Hylas, and pulled him down into the spring.

33

His friends afterwards found the empty pitcher by the waterside, but Hylas was never seen again.

Arethusa was a wood nymph who was fond of hunting. One day, warm from the chase, she stepped into a river to cool herself, but a voice spoke to her. She was frightened, and tried to run away. The voice said, "Why do you fly? I am Alpheus, the god of this stream!" That made her run the faster. The god followed her, and she prayed to Artemis, who changed her into a river which sank into the ground and came out again far away in Sicily.

CHAPTER VIII

IN THE MOONLIGHT

THE moon had different names. She was called Selene or Artemis. As Artemis she was a mighty hunter and the friend of hunters. She and Apollo, the sun-god, were twins, and their mother was Latona.

It is said that Latona was once going on a long journey, carrying her children in her arms. She reached the country of Lycia, very tired and thirsty. In a valley she saw a number of people gathering willows on the banks of a pond where the clear water sparkled in the sunlight.

She knelt down to drink, but the countrymen stopped her.

"You cannot drink here," they said.

"Why not?" she asked. "It is true I am a stranger here, but water, like the air and light, is free to all. Why should you prevent me from drinking when my thirst is so great? See, I ask it of you as a favor. I will not bathe in it, but only cool my parched throat. That will not rob you, for there is plenty. Even my poor children stretch their hands to plead with you for this mercy."

But the rude and unkind people said, "No! You are a foreigner. Your dress is strange; you do not talk as we do. Where do you come from with these children? You should have stayed in your own country and drunk its waters. This pond is ours, and it is not for you."

To make sure that she should not drink, they waded into the pond, and with their feet stirred up the mud from the bottom. Latona was angry, and she prayed to the gods in heaven.

"O ye gods!" she said, "if there is any among you who pities a poor mother and her helpless children thus wronged, hear my prayer! Grant that these cold-blooded wretches may never leave that pond, but live there, they and their children after them, forever."

A change came over the men in the pool. Their mouths stretched very wide, and out of them came harsh, croaking voices. Their heads joined their bodies without any neck between. Their breasts turned white and their backs green, and their legs grew very slim. Some jumped out upon the bank of the pond, but soon jumped in again. Some swam in the water, others dived into the mud. They were no longer men; they had become frogs.

The story of Endymion is very different. He kept a flock of sheep upon Mount Latmos, and in the quiet nights of summer, when the moon was shining brightly, he delighted in singing to the moon, whose light he loved. One evening he saw before him a charming young woman, as he supposed. Her belt and sandals were silver, and in her hand she carried a silver bow. A diamond sparkled like a star upon her forehead. At the same moment the moon had gone behind a cloud, but the young woman herself seemed to shine all over.

The shepherd was surprised but not afraid. "Fair creature," he said, "you wander late upon the mountain side."

"Yes," she answered; "it is my duty, as it is yours to keep sheep."

"But you are a stranger here," said Endymion. "I have seen all the daughters of the shepherds upon this mountain, and you are not one of them."

"The daughter of a shepherd! No!" she replied. "Yet you have often looked upon my face."

"Pardon me!" he returned. "Your dress and manner show me that you are at least the daughter of a king, and if I had ever seen you I could not have forgotten."

"You have not only seen me, but you have sung to me. Many a night I have heard you praising me when flocks and men were wrapped in sleep and only you and I were awake."

Then Endymion knew that this was Artemis, the moon goddess.

"Have my poor songs made you angry?" he asked.

"Oh, no!" she answered. "They have pleased me

so much that I have come to thank you and to ask what you most desire, that I may grant it to you."

"Bright goddess!" he cried, "I do not want to grow old. Grant that I may be forever young."

"For that," she replied, "I must ask the king and father of the gods. For to-night farewell. To-morrow evening we shall meet again."

Then she vanished, but the moon smiled all night on the mountain side.

The next night she came again, but her face was sad.

"I have brought your gift," she said, "but I am sorry you asked it. The king of heaven commands that you shall be forever young, but that you must forever sleep."

"Alas!" he cried. "Then I can see you no more, you whom I love!"

His eyes closed, he sank down upon the grass. The Greeks believed that he lay somewhere on top of Latmos, and that the moon-goddess watched over his long sleep. Every night when her bright light shone on the mountain the people said, "Artemis is smiling upon Endymion."

ENDYMION

CHAPTER IX

AMONG THE STARS

T HE Greeks did not know that the stars were worlds, but fancied that they were the homes of bright spirits who once had lived on earth. In fact, they often spoke as if the stars were the spirits themselves.

In the northern sky are seven bright stars arranged in a peculiar order, which have been noticed and admired from very early times.

These are sometimes call the "Dipper," but they are part of a group named the "Great Bear."

It was said that Hera was angry with a woman called Callisto and changed her into a bear. Instead of being beautiful she became frightful, and dogs and hunters chased her through the forest. She still kept her human knowledge and feelings, and was afraid, not only of the hunters, but of the wild beasts among whom she must live. For many years she remained in that miserable condition.

When she lived among mankind she had a son whom she dearly loved; but when she was a bear she did not dare go near him. He had grown up, when she met him one day in the woods, and ran toward him, forgetting that she was a wild beast.

The lad was afraid, and was just about to kill her with his hunting spear. Zeus, who saw this, was sorry for both. He caught them up into heaven and set them there. The mother is the "Great Bear," and another smaller group of stars near by is called the "Little Bear."

These stars move always around the North Pole, and never set in the ocean as other stars seem to do. The last star in the tail of the Little Bear is the Polar Star.

Poseidon had a son named Orion. He was a giant and very fond of hunting. His father had taught him how to walk under water, or, as some say, on the water.

He loved Merope, daughter of the king of Chios, who told him that he must clear that island of wild beasts before he could claim his bride. Orion went into the forest every day, and at night carried to the king the skins of the beasts he had killed. When there were no more wolves or bears on the island, he said, "Now, give me your daughter."

But the king made so many excuses that Orion tried to carry off the girl. Her father was angry. He gave wine to Orion, and, when he had taken too much, blinded him with hot irons, and threw him out on the seashore.

When he came to himself he wandered around

until he heard the noise of a hammer. He followed it and came to the place where Hephæstus was working. The blacksmith was sorry for the poor blind giant, and sent a man to lead him into the sun. They went eastward until they met Apollo, who gave Orion his sight again.

He then became a hunter for Artemis. She loved him and would have married him, but her brother, the sun-god, did not like that, and determined to prevent it. One day he saw Orion wading in the sea with his head just out of water.

"Sister," said Apollo, "you think you are a good shot with your arrows."

"Yes, I am," she said.

"Well, do you see that black thing bobbing up and down in the sea? I don't believe you can hit that in three trials."

"You shall see," cried Artemis. She shot one arrow, and the black thing disappeared. After a while the waves rolled poor Orion to the shore. Artemis was very sorry, but she could not bring back his life. She could only set him among the stars, where he shines on winter nights. Three bright stars are his belt. Look up into the sky any clear night in December, and you can see his belt, and, hanging below it, his sword.

His dog, Sirius, is at his heels, and the Pleiades fly before him. They were seven sisters who hunted with Artemis. One day in his lifetime Orion chased them, and they prayed to the gods for help. Zeus changed them into pigeons, but afterward set them into the sky as a group of stars. We can only see six now, because, it is said, one of them could not bear to look down and see the burning city of Troy. Her son had founded that city, and she was so sorry for its ruin that she went away, and since then has never been seen. She is called "The Lost Pleiad." Her sisters were so grieved that since then they have shone with a paler light.

There is another group of stars, called the Hyades, of which this story was told. When the god of wine, Dionysus, or Bacchus, was a little child, his mother, Semele, died, and he was left helpless. A family of sisters pitied him, and took care of him until he was grown up. The king of the gods was greatly pleased with their kindness, and to reward them took them up to heaven, and made them shine like stars. They are often called "the rainy Hyades."

Other constellations or clusters of stars were supposed to be shaped like animals. Not only were there two bears, but also a lion, a bull, a ram, a goat, a crab, a scorpion, and two fishes. Among these the sun journeyed every day, though his bright light hid them from human eyes.

CHAPTER X

THE KINGDOM UNDER THE GROUND

THE Greeks thought that there was a kingdom underground over which a king reigned whom they called Dis. We generally call him by his other name of Pluto.

It was a very gloomy world, full of dark caves, and with black rivers rolling through dimly lighted plains. On one of the rivers was a boat rowed by Charon, who met the dead as they came down from the upper world, and ferried them across the wide stream. He would only take into his boat those who had been properly buried. Those who had been drowned, or had fallen in battle and lain neglected on the battlefield, or any who had perished on mountains or in deserts, were left to wander up and down the gloomy banks of the black river. They had no home either in the world above or the world below. For that reason the Greeks were very particular to give their friends a good funeral. Generally dead bodies were burned, and their ashes gathered up and buried.

These dead people were only shades, or shadows,

44

or ghosts, very thin and pale, and with faint, weak voices. Some were punished for their sins. Ixion was fastened to a wheel which turned around forever. Sisyphus rolled uphill a heavy stone, which as soon as it reached the top rolled down again, so that his labor never ended. Tantalus stood in water up to the chin, but when he bent his head to drink, the water flowed away out of his reach. Over his head hung branches with apples, pears and grapes, but when he stretched up his hand to gather them they drew away, so that he was forever hungry and thirsty. He was always "tantalized," as we say.

Those who had been good and who had done good while on the earth were happier, but not very happy.

Cerberus, the watchdog of this place, kept the shades from escaping. He was glad to see those who came in, but tore in pieces those who tried to run away. He had three heads, and every hair on his body was a snake.

King Dis, or Pluto, had a black chariot with four black horses. Once he took a ride up to this sunlit world of ours. He came to a valley filled with lilies and violets, and among them, fairer and sweeter than any, was a young girl filling a basket with the flowers. Pluto was very lonely in his dark home. He had no queen to cheer and comfort him. When he saw this girl he thought, "How bright she would make that old palace of mine!"

He sent a servant to catch her and bring her to the chariot. Then he set out for home. Persephone—her Latin name was Proserpina—screamed and cried, but the king drove on and down, and made her queen of the underworld.

This girl was the daughter of Demeter, the earth-mother, who went everywhere seeking her child. As she went she wept. The peasants did not know who she was, but they pitied her and said, "Good woman, come into our hut, eat bread and drink milk."

But she said, "How can I eat unless I find my child? Have you seen her?"

They could only sadly answer, "No!"

She went on and on, asking the flowers, the trees, the rivers, the stars, the men and women and wandering gods whom she met, if they had seen her child. They had only one answer, "No. We have not seen her."

One woman asked, "Was she very beautiful?"

"Oh," said the weeping mother, "she was most beautiful! No star was brighter, no flower was sweeter, no bird had a more musical voice. If you had seen her you would know. Earth had not her like, and heaven itself had nothing lovelier."

The woman said, "No, I have not seen her. My own little daughter is very pretty. Did you notice her?" But Demeter had no eyes for other children, so she went on and on, over land and sea, calling, "Persephone! My child, my darling! Are you forever lost to me?"

She reached Sicily, and found the place where Pluto had gone down with Persephone. She cried, "O wicked and ungrateful earth! I have made thee rich and beautiful with grass and grain, and yet thou openest a

46

way for a monster to carry off my daughter. Thou shalt no more be fruitful, only thorns and thistles shall grow upon thy breast."

Arethusa, the river-goddess, said to her, "Do not be cruel, good mother. I came through the underworld and saw your daughter there. She is the queen and is so afraid, but whether or not she is happy I do not know."

When Demeter heard that, she went up instantly to Zeus and asked him to get back her daughter.

The king of the gods said, "If she has not eaten anything down there, she can be set free. But if she has taken any of their food she must stay."

Hermes was sent down to bring her back, if possible. He asked her if she had eaten anything that grew in the underworld.

"Nothing," she said, "except a few pomegranate seeds, but they were very few."

Pluto said, "I claim my rights. You see she has eaten here, and she must stay with me."

Hermes argued with the dark king, who said, "Her mother loves her dearly. So do I. Why must I give her up? It was very lonely here before she came. I cannot live that way again."

Hermes said, "Do this! Let her mother have her for six months; then she shall come back and stay with you for six months."

It was arranged that way. In the spring and

summer, when the flowers were blooming, Persephone lived with her mother, and they went hand in hand through the fields. Through dark autumn and gloomy winter she sat on the throne by Pluto, and made the shadowy underworld brighter and happier.

CHAPTER XI

SOWING DRAGON'S TEETH

P HŒNICIA was a kingdom on the eastern shore of the Mediterranean Sea. Its king had a daughter named Europa, who went out one day and never came home. Some said that Zeus had taken her, others declared that pirates had carried her off in their ship.

The king called his sons together and said, "Without your sister the palace is dark and my heart is broken. Go through the world and find her. Do not come back without her, for you will not be welcome."

The young men scattered in all directions. They did not find their sister, but found wives in different lands where they settled. One of the brothers, named Cadmus, went to the oracle of Apollo and asked where he should make his home. The oracle told him to follow a cow until she stopped, and there he should build a city and call it Thebes.

Cadmus went out from the cave, and saw a cow before him. She walked along very slowly, stopping only for a minute to eat a mouthful of grass, then going on again until the youth was nearly tired out. Finally she came to a broad plain, where she lay down.

Cadmus was glad and thankful. He needed some pure water for a sacrifice, perhaps to drink. He told his servants to go and find a spring. They found one in a thick grove where was a cave overgrown with bushes, and from it a clear stream of sparkling water flowed out.

As the servants dipped their pitchers, they heard a frightful hiss. At the same moment a terrible head came out of the cave,—a dragon's head. The dragon had a body like a snake, covered with scales like a fish. Its claws were those of a lion, its head had a beak like that of an eagle, and its teeth were like those of any wild beast. It breathed out fire and smoke, and was altogether a dreadful thing to meet.

The strangers from Phœnica stood still with surprise and fright. The dragon struck some with its claws, crushed some with its teeth, stifled others with its breath and strangled in its coils those who were left.

Cadmus waited a long time, but his men did not return. He followed them and found a fiery dragon. A battle began between them, but the man kept his spear always at the dragon's mouth so that the monster could not reach him. He already wounded the creature, and by one strong push of the spear he fastened its head to a tree.

When it was dead he heard a voice say, "Sow the dragon's teeth! Sow the dragon's teeth!" He took the sharp white teeth out of the jaws and planted them

CADMUS AND THE DRAGON

in the ground. In a few minutes armed men began to come up out of the earth. They had shields, breastplates, helmets and swords. Some had bows and arrows.

As soon as they saw each other, they began to fight savagely. Cadmus expected them to turn upon him, but they never looked at him.

They struck and shot and stabbed each other until only five were left. One of these said, "Stop! We are all brothers, why should we fight any more? Let us live in peace!"

Then turning to Cadmus he added, "You have brought us here. What shall we do to serve you?"

Cadmus was glad to see them peaceable. He said, "The oracle told me to build a city here. I cannot do it alone, and the dragon destroyed my servants. If you will help me I shall be very glad."

They answered, "You are our master. What you command we perform."

They very willingly helped to build the city, which was not very large at first, but grew in time to be rich and splendid.

Cadmus is said to have taught the Greeks the alphabet which was used at his old home in Phœnicia. Before he went to Greece, there were no books in that land, and nobody wrote a letter, for nobody could read one. Instead of written histories, men told their children what their own grandfathers had told them. Poets carried their verses in their memories, or made them up as they went along. There were no schools and no teachers, except that every father taught his boys how to farm and to fight, and girls learned from their mothers how to spin and weave and sew.

The coming of Cadmus made a great difference. First men learned to write, then to read, for no one can read when nothing is written. After books came schools, and Greek civilization and learning went on together.

CHAPTER XII

THE RACE OF ATALANTA

ATALANTA was a young and beautiful girl who lived near the city of Thebes. She asked an oracle to tell her fortune, and was answered that she must never marry, for if she did she would be most unhappy. She turned away from the company of young men, and found her pleasure in hunting. Life in the open air made her stronger and still more beautiful, and she learned to run more swiftly than any youth, or any other maiden, in her native country.

Young men heard of her loveliness, and went to ask her in marriage. "I do not wish to be married," she said, "Whoever would have me for his wife must run a race with me, but I warn you that every one who fails in that race must die."

These were hard terms, but some were willing to take the risk for the chance of gaining such a charming wife. None could run like Atalanta, and several lost their lives in the vain effort to win her.

A youth named Hippomenes was chosen to be judge of one of these races. He consented to act, thinking at the same time that any man was foolish to risk his life for the sake of a woman.

When he saw the girl, young, strong, swift, and lovely, he changed his mind.

The race was run. Atalanta seemed to have wings. Youth after youth was left behind. She had no pity on any. Whoever failed must pay the dreadful price.

Hippomenes said, "Why do you boast of having beaten such laggards as those? I myself will race with you, and I know that I shall win."

Atalanta looked at him, and for the first time her heart felt pity. She was sure that she could not be beaten by any mortal, and she was sorry that such a handsome young man would wish to put his life in danger.

Orders were given to prepare for the race. Hippomenes did not mean to be beaten, so he prayed to Aphrodite. "O goddess!" he said, "thou hast impelled me to undertake this race. Grant me thy help that I may win the maiden."

Aphrodite was pleased, and willing to aid her worshiper. She took three golden apples from the garden of her temple at Cyprus, and gave them to Hippomenes. "Use these as I tell you," she said. "They will win you the victory."

The race began. The two ran very close together, but Hippomenes was a step ahead. He threw down one of the golden apples, but the girl only glanced at it, and ran as rapidly as ever.

He threw another apple. She seemed about to

stoop for it, but changed her mind and ran on. Then Hippomenes threw his last apple, and the temptation proved too strong for the maiden. She turned aside a little, bent down swiftly, and seized the apple, and in that moment Hippomenes threw himself forward, and touched the goal with two fingers.

Atalanta had lost, and Hippomenes became her husband. They were very glad and happy together, but in their joy they forgot to sacrifice to Aphrodite. She aroused against them the anger of Cybele, who was regarded by some nations as the great mother of all the gods. That goddess changed them from human into beastly forms. To Atalanta she gave the shape of a lioness, to Hippomenes that of a lion. She yoked them to her car, and in all paintings or statues of Cybele she is shown as drawn by these unhappy lovers, for whom the oracle was sadly fulfilled.

CHAPTER XIII

MEN TURNED TO STONE

THE king of Argos was angry and afraid. An oracle had told him that he should die by the hand of his daughter's child. He shut up his daughter and her little boy in a box, and pushed them off to sea.

They floated to an island, Seriphos, where a fisherman found them and took them to his home.

After a while, Polydectes, the king of the island, wanted to get rid of the boy, Perseus, that he might marry Danae, the mother. He sent the lad, who was then well grown, to find and bring back the head of Medusa. She was the Gorgon, one of three sisters who had teeth like those of swine, brass claws, wings like those of eagles, and hair which was hissing snakes. The others were ugly enough, but Medusa was so frightful that any living thing that looked on her was turned into stone. Perseus was to cut off her head and take it home to the king.

He could never have done that if Athene and Hermes had not helped him. The goddess lent him

57

her bright shield, and he borrowed from Hermes his winged shoes and crooked sword.

He flew far and farther until he came to the land where Medusa and her sisters lay asleep. Using the bright shield as a mirror, so that he did not look at Medusa but at her image, he flew down, and with one sudden stroke cut off her head. He put it into his wallet and rose from the ground just as the other sisters wakened. They flew after him for a long time, but could not catch one who wore the winged shoes of Hermes.

After several days of flying Perseus reached the country of the Æthiopians. Here he found sorrow and weeping. The queen of that land has boasted that she was more beautiful than the sea nymphs. To punish her they sent a monster of the sea to swim up and down the Æthiopian coast. It sunk the ships and ate the crews. Nobody could go fishing, or sailing, or bathing, because of this monster.

The king and queen went to the oracle, which said, "Chain your daughter Andromeda to a rock in the sea, and let the monster have her. It will then go away, and your country will be free."

At the moment when Perseus arrived she was chained to the rock and waiting to be eaten by the monster. The young hero flew down near her and said, "O, maiden, why do you weep, and why are you thus chained at the edge of the sea?"

She told him, and the crowds that lined the shore wept while she spoke. Her father and mother were there, and above all others their cries were heard.

Perseus said, "I will try to save her from the monster."

The sea serpent came swimming, making a loud noise, and with its head high above the waves. Perseus flew up in the air, came down on the monster's back, and struck a blow with the crooked sword. When the dragon darted head or claws at him, he flew up out of reach; then, coming down suddenly, struck again and again. The monster lost its strength, and sank slowly under the water. The people waited and watched, but it did not rise again.

Andromeda was unbound, and the king and queen with Perseus and all the people went, filled with joy, to the palace.

While they were feasting a number of young men burst in. One of them said, "I have come to claim my bride."

The king said, "Why did you not rescue her when she was in danger? I shall give her to the stranger who saved her life."

A fight began which was settled by Perseus. "Let every friend of mine turn away his eyes and not look at me!" he cried. He drew out the Gorgon's head and held it up. Every one of the attacking party looked at it, and all were turned to stone.

Perseus took his young wife to Seriphos, the island where lived the king who had sent him on his search for the head of Medusa. He went into the royal dining hall. The king laughed at him and asked, "Did you bring the Gorgon's head?" The company thought that a very good joke, and laughed heartily.

The king had been very cruel to the mother of Perseus. The young man was angry for that reason, and when the company mocked at him he opened his wallet and took out the dreadful head. "Look," he said. They turned toward him, and were changed into stone.

Perseus journeyed through a country where the young men were holding games. His grandfather, Acrisius, whom Perseus did not know, was looking on. Perseus joined the game and threw a quoit. It went far, and fell heavily on the foot of the old man. He fainted with pain and was carried from the field. In a short time he died. So the oracle was fulfilled, and he died by the hand of his daughter's son.

Perseus was very sorry, but he was entirely innocent, and that was a comfort. He gave the Gorgon's head to Athene, who set it in the middle of her shining shield. The sword and shoes were given back to Hermes. Perseus did not fly abroad any more, but stayed at home with Andromeda.

CHAPTER XIV

BLACK SAILS OR WHITE

WHEN Ægeus, prince of Athens, was a young man he traveled in other countries, in one of which he met and married a young woman.

They were very happy until word came that Ægeus must go to Athens and be king. His father was dead, and the people called for him.

His wife and little boy went a short way on the journey with him. The prince took off his sword and shoes and hid them under a heavy stone by the roadside.

"When our boy is strong enough to lift that stone, let him bring the sword and shoes to me at Athens," he said and went forward. The wife and child turned back to their own city.

The little boy's name was Theseus. When he had grown up his mother took him to the stone and said, "My son, do you think that you could roll away that stone?"

He did so easily. There lay a sword and shoes. "What are these?" he asked.

His mother said, "They are yours. Once they belonged to your father. Take them to him in Athens, and he will know that you are his son."

Theseus went overland and met and overcame many dangers. At one place he found a strong and cruel man called Procrustes, which means the "Stretcher." He had an iron bedstead on which he made every passer-by lie down. If any were too short, he stretched their legs to make them long enough. When any were too long, he cut off their feet and ankles until they just fitted. Only those who were exactly the right length could go unharmed.

Theseus conquered this wretch, broke up the bedstead, and threw the pieces into the sea.

At Athens he showed the sword and shoes to the king, who asked, "How did you get these?"

"My mother showed me where they were hidden under a stone. I lifted it and took them," was the answer.

"These were mine before they were yours. I am your father, and you are my princely son," said the king.

Theseus found the Athenians in great trouble. At that season in every year they had to send to Crete seven young men and seven maidens to feed the Minotaur. This was a monster with the body of a bull, the head of a man, and the teeth of a lion. He was kept in a place called a labyrinth, which had so many rooms, doors and passages that no one who went in could ever find the way out without help. Minos, the king of Crete, loved this monster and fed him on human beings.

When the ship was ready to carry the young people away, Theseus went on board as one of the victims. The sails were black because everybody was mourning. Theseus had a set of white sails with him, and said to the king, "Father, watch for the ship. If she comes home in black you will know I have failed. If she carries white sails you may be sure that I have succeeded."

When they reached Crete the young people were taken up to the palace that the king might see them. His daughter, Ariadne, was sorry for them all, but most sorry for Theseus. She liked him and determined to save him. That night, she carried him a sword and a ball of thread.

She told him, "You must go first into the labyrinth; the others must follow you. Take the sword with you, and keep the ball of thread in your left hand, so that it will unwind as you go. I will hold one end outside the labyrinth. When you wish to come out, wind the thread up carefully, and follow it to the outer door."

In the morning Theseus did exactly as she had said. He went far into the labyrinth and saw the Minotaur coming toward him. He gave the ball of thread to one of the young men and said, "Keep out of this fight. If I am killed run as fast as you can, winding up the thread as you go. You and the others may escape in that way.

If I win, stand still and give me back the ball. I will lead you out."

By this time the Minotaur came up, bellowing, and pawing the ground.

The battle began, and the young Athenians trembled as they watched the fight. The monster was strong and quick, but Theseus was quicker, and his sword was very sharp. After an hour or so of hard fighting the Minotaur was weakened, and fell to his knees. Theseus with one swift blow cut off his head, and the danger was over.

He wound up the clew, as the ball of thread was called, and it led him and his young friends out into freedom. Ariadne was waiting for them.

"You must hurry to your ship and get away," she said. "My father will be very angry, and you are not safe one moment while you stay."

"Will you go with us?" asked Theseus.

"Yes," she said, "for my father will be just as angry with me."

They reached their ship and were soon on the open sea. They stopped at the island of Naxos and left Ariadne there. She afterwards married Dionysus, the god of wine.

When the ship drew near the shore of Attica, the old king was watching from the top of a high rock directly above the sea. He saw a vessel coming, but, alas, her sails were black! In his joy, Theseus had forgotten to change the sails from black to white. The poor father

ÆGEUS, WATCHING FOR THE SHIP

thought his son was dead, and fell fainting into the sea. Ever afterward it was called, in memory of him, the Ægean Sea.

CHAPTER XV

WINGS OF WAX

THE man who built the labyrinth for King Minos was named Dædalus. He was a genius and could do wonderful things. The king became angry at him and shut him up in a tower. He easily escaped, but could not leave the island of Crete because the king watched all the ships, and no captain dared take Dædalus on board.

He put together sticks of strong but light wood, and made a pair of frames. On these he fastened feathers with wax and cord until they were like the wings of a very large bird. He made another and smaller pair for his son Icarus, who was always playing around him and asking questions.

When all was ready he took the boy to the top of a high hill near the sea. First he arranged the smaller pair of wings upon his son, then fitted the larger pair to his own shoulders and arms. He thought best to give Icarus some good advice.

"My son," he said, "we are now about to try a strange and wonderful thing. I believe these wings are strong enough to bear us safely across the sea into another and more friendly land, but I warn you to be careful. When we are once in the air I can do little to help you. Follow me and keep near me. Do just what I do, and it is my hope that all will be well."

The boy promised to obey. His father threw him upward a little way; he spread his wings, and found that he could really fly. Dædalus sprang up, darted past him, and said again, "Follow me closely, my son!"

It was wonderful and delightful. High in air, but not too high, they sailed over the land like gigantic birds. Farmers stopped their plows and looked up with open mouths. Cattle lifted their heads and started at the strange sight. Women going to the wells for water ran screaming home. Boys and men took their bows and shot arrows which could not reach the fliers.

Soon they were over the sea. The blue waters sparkled below them. Fisherman left their nets, and rowers dropped their oars, to wonder at the huge birds that cast such a wide shadow.

Icarus had never been so happy. He was not the least afraid, for he could manage his wings perfectly. His father was pleased to see him keeping so near and doing so well.

Like other boys, this one got tired of being safe and happy. Suddenly he shot up into the air, higher and higher. He could see much farther and was proud of his daring. He grew very warm, for the sun was shining with great heat. The wax upon his wings began to melt. It dripped away, carrying the feathers with it. The bare frames could not hold him up. He was no longer a bird; he was nothing but a boy.

He fell. His father could not catch him, and if he had caught him, one pair of wings was not enough for two persons.

Icarus fell into the sea. The spray leaped up, the waves danced. That was all.

His father flew down to a land which was close by, and which he called Icaria, in memory of his foolish and disobedient son.

Dædalus had a nephew Perdix, whom he taught to be a skillful workman. This boy picked up on the seashore the back-bone of a fish. Looking at it gave him an idea. He took a piece of iron, made notches in the edge, and thus invented the saw.

He took two pieces of iron, sharpened them at one end, riveted them together at the other, and made the first pair of compasses.

Dædalus was not pleased. He thought the boy was a greater genius than himself, and that was unbearable. He took Perdix to the top of a high tower and pushed him off. He would surely have been killed if Athene had not been watching him. She changed him into the bird called the partridge, which builds its nest on the ground, and never flies high in the air because it knows the danger of falling.

CHAPTER XVI

THE GOOD SHIP ARGO

"I AM tired of going to school," said Jason. "I am a man now, and I shall go and claim my kingdom from my uncle." His father had been a king, but had given up his kingdom to his half-brother. "Keep it until my son is of age," he said. "When he is old enough to reign, yield him the throne as now I yield it to you." The brother promised, but never meant to keep his word.

Jason had been put to Chiron's school. Chiron was a centaur; that is, he had a man's head and chest and arms, joined to the body and four legs of a horse. He was an excellent teacher and had many famous pupils.

Jason dressed for his journey, put on a pair of handsome sandals that had belonged to his father, said farewell to teacher, and fellow-pupils, and set out to gain his kingdom.

On the way he came to a wide river running very swiftly. On the bank stood a feeble, poor old woman, who was wringing her hands and saying, "Oh, I must get over! Who will help me over?"

Jason was not very willing but he had been taught at school to always be kind to the poor and old, in fact to everybody who needed help. So he knelt down and said, "Climb on my back, good mother, and I will carry you over if I can."

She got on his broad young shoulders, and he plunged into the stream. Its bed was very rocky and uneven, and the rushing current was very powerful, but he fought his way through, and put down the old woman on the other side. She thanked him kindly, but he was vexed to see that one of his feet was bare because he had lost a sandal in the river.

The old woman said, "Never mind, my kind young friend. Some things are better lost than found. My blessing goes with you, and it may bring you good fortune."

This was really the goddess Hera, but Jason did not know it until afterwards.

He went on and reached the city where his uncle held his court. People looked at the lad with wonder, as he limped along the streets with one foot shod and the other bare. Some began to call after him, "One sandal! One sandal! See the man with one sandal!" The cry rang through the city, and the king heard it in his palace.

An oracle had once told him to beware of a man with one sandal. He sent a servant to bring this stranger before him.

"Who are you?" the king asked, "and what are you doing in my kingdom?"

"If you are Pelias," answered the youth, "I am your nephew. My name is Jason; this is my kingdom, and I have come to claim my rights."

The king replied, "If you are a king you must do kingly deeds. If you will go and bring me the Golden Fleece, you will prove yourself a hero, and the kingdom shall be yours."

Jason was pleased with the thought. "I shall need a ship and men," he said. His uncle replied, "The best shipbuilder in the world lives here. His name is Argus. I will give you money for the vessel; you can easily find men."

Jason went to the oracle of the speaking oak at Dodona, and it told him to hire Argus to build the vessel. He cut off a bough of the oak and took it to Argus.

"Here," he said, "is the first timber of a ship I wish you to build for me. It must be long and strong, with room for fifty rowers. This branch you must put into the prow, that it may always see where we are going and warn us of danger."

No such large vessel had ever yet been built. But Argus went to work upon her, and, while he was busy, Jason sent out heralds to all the cities of Greece, telling of his large ship, and inviting brave young men to join him in the search for the Golden Fleece.

Many were willing to go. They went to the city where Jason was, and waited until the new ship was finished. She was called "Argo," after her builder. When she was ready they all laid hold upon her and pushed and pulled, trying to launch her. But she did not move; she was too heavy.

They were almost in despair when Jason thought of the oak branch. "Child of Dodona," he cried, "you see how helpless we are. Tell us what to do!"

The branch answered, "Take your place at the oars, and let Orpheus play upon his harp."

Orpheus was a famous musician, of whom we shall presently learn more.

The Argonauts, as they were called, went on board and took their oars; fifty rowers sitting in a boat under forest trees far from the water. Orpheus lifted his harp and struck the strings. The ship gave a little leap and started for the sea. Out of the woods and down the shore she went, Orpheus playing all the way, until the bow struck the water, the spray dashed over the oak branch, and the big ship was afloat.

CHAPTER XVII

THE GOLDEN FLEECE

THE Argo was headed for Colchis, where the Golden Fleece was kept in a sacred grove. The first danger her crew had to meet was at the opening of the Euxine or Black Sea, where two islands floated about, sometimes knocking against each other and crushing everything caught between them. When these clashing rocks were reached the sailors let go a dove they had on their ship. She flew between the islands and only lost one or two tail-feathers. Jason seized the favorable moment of the rebound. The crew rowed hard and pulled the ship through with very little damage.

At Colchis the king said they could have the Golden Fleece, but there were two or three little things that must be done first. He had two bulls whose feet were brass and whose breath were fire. Would Jason kindly yoke them to a plow?

Then there were the teeth of that dragon which Cadmus had killed. If they were sown, armed men would be the harvest. Would Jason like to do a little farming of that kind?

Jason said that he had no objection. He would do anything necessary to get the Fleece. A day was fixed for these trials, and Jason went away from the palace.

In the garden he met the king's daughter, Medea. She was young and handsome, but she was a powerful witch. She liked the young stranger and promised to help him. She taught him some magic words to say and gave him a charm that would conquer everything.

On the day of the trial the king had a throne set up in the field, and crowds were standing around. The keeper of the bulls let them go, and they came rushing into the open space where Jason stood. When they drew near he spoke the magic words. The bulls stopped short. They did not paw the ground, and their breath was not quite so fiery. Jason walked up to them, spoke kindly to them, patted their sides, and slipped a yoke over their necks. He led them quietly to the plow, hitched them up, and plowed the field.

A servant handed him the dragon's teeth, and he sowed them in the furrows. Men sprung up with helmets on their heads, shields on their left arms, and swords in their right hands. They came at Jason, who fought them for a little while, but finding them too many picked up a stone and threw it among them. Immediately they left Jason and began to fight among themselves. When the battle was over, not one of them was living.

The king was not pleased, but told the heroes that they should have the Golden Fleece the next day. That night Medea came to them as they were sleeping at

THE FIERY BULLS

their ship, and told them that her father meant to bring an army in the morning and burn the Argo.

There was moonlight that night, and Jason and Medea went together to the grove where the Golden Fleece was hanging. This was the skin of a ram which Hermes had given to a woman to help her save her two children from another woman who hated them. The children were placed on the back of the ram, which started off through the air. As they were crossing the Dardanelles, between Asia and Europe, the little girl, Helle, fell into the sea, which was afterwards called the Hellespont, or Helle's Sea. The boy held on, and the ram carried him to Colchis. The beast was sacrificed to Zeus, and its skin with the golden wool was hung up in a sacred grove. A dragon was set to watch it, and he never slept.

Medea began to walk around and around before him, singing and waving her hands, and throwing over him a drug that would make him sleep. To his own great surprise the dragon began to nod. First one eye shut, then the other, then both. They opened again quickly, but only for a little while. There was that strange young woman who made him dizzy with her walk and sleepy with her song. A pleasant smell came from the cool liquid with which she sprinkled him. The dragon shut his eyes and opened his mouth. He did not speak, he snored. He laid his heavy head down on the grass. Jason stepped over him, took the Golden Fleece, threw it over his shoulders, and hurried with Medea to the ship. The rowers pushed off from the shore and rowed away for

Thessaly. Jason took his kingdom and lived, a good ruler, for many years.

Jason's father was old and weak. The hero wanted him to be younger and stronger. He said to Medea, "My dear wife, you can do many things. Can you take some years of mine and add them to my father's life?"

"I can do better than that," she answered. "I can make his life longer, but yours need not be shorter."

She went out at night and said wonderful words to the moon, the stars, and all the gods of woods and caves, of rivers and winds. A chariot drawn by flying serpents came through the air and landed at her feet. She stepped into it and rode far away to gather strange herbs. This she did for nine nights until she had enough for her use. She lit a fire and boiled the herbs with many other strange things. Where the liquid bubbled over and fell on the ground, a dry olive branch which it touched was covered with leaves and olives, and the grass grew greener and stronger.

Jason laid his father down on a bed of soft herbs, and Medea cut the old man's throat. When all his blood was gone she poured in the magic liquid. As it filled his veins, his white hair and beard turned black, his pale and wrinkled face grew smooth and rosy, his limbs were round and strong. He stood up and said, "I am young again. I shall be twenty-one to-morrow."

CHAPTER XVIII

LOST BY LOOKING BACK

APOLLO had a son named Orpheus, who was a great musician. His lyre, or small harp, was a present from his father, who taught him how to play upon it, so that it charmed all who heard. When he played in the woods the trees began to dance, rather stiffly to be sure. When he passed near rocks with his lyre they did not exactly melt, but their hard hearts were softened. The savage beasts lost their fierceness, and the timid ones laid aside their fears. They came out from their dens and followed him, lions and tigers, wolves and rabbits, bears and stags.

In his youth he was one of the crew of the ship Argo, and at his playing the vessel launched herself. He married Eurydice, and they were very happy, but one day she trod upon a snake hidden in the grass. It bit her in the foot, and she died.

Her husband's music changed entirely. Before that he sang of hope and joy and peace and love. Now his only song was one of sorrow for his great loss.

He thought if he went down to the underworld

he might coax Pluto to let him have his wife again. He found a deep cave and went down and down, until through the deep darkness he saw a dim light. He knew that he had reached the kingdom of the dead. He played to old Charon and sang of his dead wife, until the boatman said, "Come aboard! I will take you over!"

He went up to the palace and found king Pluto and his queen. He played upon his lyre and sang to them.

"Oh, you, who love each other and are happy," he said, "think of my grief and pity my sorrow. She who was the light of my eyes is in darkness here. She who made me happy goes lonely here among these pale ghosts, while I walk mourning upon the earth. When I sang her sweet voice answered me; now I hear it no more. Others praised me, but her praise was dearer than that of all beside.

"I do not come to break up your kingdom. She has died before her time. We must all come to you, O mighty king! If you give her back to me now, she and I must soon return to this world of shadows. But spare her to me, that we may be happy for a while. Fair queen, speak for me to your dark lord. Remember how your mother went sorrowing for you, and have pity on me in my grief."

Persephone turned to her husband. Her face was wet with tears. "O king and lord," she said, "grant this poor mortal's prayer! We are sorry to be parted from each other for six months when I go to my mother. How sad it must be when parting is forever!"

80

Tears rolled down the thin cheeks of many ghosts. The king said, "Mortal, on one condition you may have your wife again. She must follow you to the upper world, and you must not look upon her until you are both in the clear light of day."

Orpheus was glad indeed. He thanked the king and queen and went to the river. Charon ferried him and Eurydice across, and they began to climb upward through dark caves. They could speak to each other, and that was pleasant for them and kept them cheerful. When they had gone a long way Orpheus saw a faint light far ahead. They were almost in safety. Eurydice could only follow slowly, for, ghost as she was, her foot hurt her.

Her husband was so glad to be near the upper world that he forgot Pluto's warning. "Eurydice," he said, "Do you see the light? Are you coming?"

He looked around and saw his wife smiling, but only for a moment. "Eurydice!" he called. A weak voice answered, "Farewell! Farewell forever!" She was gone; carried back to the place of shades.

He went to the underworld again as fast as he could. She had already crossed the river. He tried to get into the boat, but Charon drove him back.

"You had your chance and lost it," the old boatman cried. "Those who cannot keep what they get must expect to lose."

For seven days Orpheus wandered up and down on the banks of the river until everybody was tired of hearing him sing and cry. Then he went back to the sunlit world. All his song was about his loss and sorrow. The maidens of Thrace pitied him and would have been glad to comfort him, but he would not listen to them. One name was on his lips, one darling was in his thoughts. "Eurydice!" he cried. "So near, so far! Lost, lost, by my own folly!"

A feast of Dionysus, or Bacchus, came on. A company of women went dancing and singing in worship of the god. "Look!" said one of them. "There is the man who hates us all!"

She threw a spear at Orpheus. He struck a few notes upon his lyre, and the spear did no harm. But the whole company of women cried out and tore their hair and ran at him. They took away his lyre, and he was powerless. With shouts and screams they beat him until he was dead, then tore him into pieces which they scattered on the river.

The Muses gathered up his remains and buried them. Zeus took the silent lyre and placed it among the stars. The song of nightingales over the musician's grave was sweeter then anywhere else in Greece.

His shade or ghost went down to the underworld. Charon said, "Now you have come to stay you may get into the boat." On the other shore Eurydice was waiting for him. Thus they were united never again to part.

CHAPTER XIX

THE HORSE WITH WINGS

IN the country of Lycia lived a monster called the Chimæra. It was part lion, part goat, and part dragon, but altogether ugly and terrible. Its breath was fire, and wherever it went the grainfields and cottages were burned. It ate cattle and people, so that the whole land groaned and trembled because of this dreadful creature.

The king was very anxious to find some hero who would kill the monster, but everybody was afraid. One day a handsome young man went to the palace and asked the king for something to do. The king told him about the Chimæra, and asked him if he would dare to meet and fight the beast. Bellerophon—that was the young man's name—said, "I am willing to try, but first I must find a wise man who can give me good advice."

They led him to an old wizard, or soothsayer, who told him, "The best thing you can do is to get the winged horse, Pegasus."

"But where shall I find him?" asked the young man.

"You must go to the temple of Athene to-night and sleep there. It may be that the goddess will appear to you and tell you what you wish to know."

Bellerophon went to the temple, and when night came lay down and slept. The goddess appeared to him in a dream and gave him a magic bridle, made of gold and precious stones. When he awoke the bridle was in his hand.

That day the kind Athene led him to a well where Pegasus was drinking. He was a beautiful horse with silver wings. He could gallop faster than any earthly horse and fly higher than any eagle.

The young man drew near to him and said, "Beautiful horse, do not fly away. Help me kill a monster which makes a whole country unhappy. See, Athene has given you this splendid bridle. No other horse ever had one so fine. Let me put it over your head."

Pegasus stood still, took the bit into his mouth, and let Bellerophon buckle the bridle. Then the youth jumped on the horse's back and said, "Now for Lycia and the Chimæra! Up, gallant steed, and make the people wonder as they see us sailing through the air."

Up they rose, and flew over mountains and rivers until they reached Lycia. They found the Chimæra in a cave. It came out hissing and spitting fire, and there was a dreadful battle. But a horse with wings could easily get out of the monster's way and fly upon him before he could turn around. First Bellerophon cut off the goat's head. The lion's head and claws fought the more savagely, but the good sword cut away that head

THE HORSE WITH WINGS

too, and then the horse with wings stamped on the dragon's body until it lay quite still. The Chimæra was conquered and killed.

Bellerophon rode proudly to the palace, and the king was glad to hear the good news. He asked Bellerophon to do a great many other hard and dangerous things, and with the help of Pegasus he did them all.

Then of course he married the king's daughter and lived very happily for a while.

But the young man grew very proud and insulting, even to the gods. He said he would fly up into heaven and live there, and nobody could hinder him. Zeus was angry and sent a gadfly to sting the horse. Pegasus gave such an unexpected jump that his rider was thrown and fell a long distance to the ground.

Friends picked him up. "You are not much hurt, Bellerophon," they said, to comfort him.

"Oh, yes!" he answered. "I cannot see, and I can hardly walk, and I have lost my horse with wings."

He wandered about in the fields lonely and blind and sorrowful, and after a while died in poverty and grief.

The horse with wings flew back to Mount Helicon where his real owners, the Muses, lived. Sometimes men caught him and kept him for a while, but he could fly away as well as run away.

Once a poet caught him and rode him for some time. But poems sold for very little money in the market, and the poet said, "I can feed neither my horse nor myself. I will sell him, and the money will buy bread for some weeks."

He took the horse to a fair and sold him to a farmer, who hitched him to a cart. He kicked the cart to pieces. They put him before a plow, but he galloped around the field and broke the plow. The farmer took a club and beat him cruelly. The horse hung his head and would not move.

The neighbors gathered around. They said, "Your horse seems balky. You were cheated when you bought him."

"Yes, yes," said the farmer. "I wish I had my good money back in my pocket."

A young man had been looking closely at the horse.

"Neighbor," he said, "let me try what I can do with this animal. Unhitch him from the plow and take off the broken harness."

This was done. The young man went to the horse's head and whispered, "By your bright eyes and wings I see you are not of common earth. Let me mount upon your back, and we will astonish these dull people."

The horse gave a soft whinny. The young man leaped on his back. Pegasus lifted his head, spread his wings, and sprang from the ground. Higher and higher they went, and while the people below stood with open eyes and mouths, Pegasus and his rider flew away to the mountain of the Muses.

CHAPTER XX

THE SINGER AND THE DOLPHIN

A T the court of the king of Corinth lived a famous musician, Arion. Everybody liked him, for he was pleasant and kind, and his music made glad all who heard it.

A musical contest was to be held in Sicily, and Arion wished to try for the prize. His friends did everything to persuade him to stay with them, but he would have his own way and sailed to Sicily.

He was the best of all the singers and won the prize. He took a Corinthian ship for home. The sky was bright, the sea was calm; he was glad to think he should soon be among his friends.

The sailors looked angrily at him. They intended to have that prize which had made him rich. They gathered around him with knives in their hands. "You must die," they said. "Make your choice. If you want to be buried on the shore, give up to us and die here. We will give you decent burial. Or throw yourself into the sea, if you would rather die that way."

Arion say, "Why should I die? You can have my gold; I will give you that. Why must you take my life?"

"Dead men tell no tales," they answered. "If we let you live you will tell the king of Corinth, and where could we hide from him? Your gold would be of no use to us, for we should always be afraid. Death quiets all. You must die."

"Grant me one favor, then," he pleaded. "If I must die, let it be as becomes a bard. So have I lived, so let me pass away. When my song is over and my harp is hushed, then I will give up my life and make no complaint."

These rough men had no pity, but they were willing to hear so great a singer. They said, "It shall be as you wish."

He added, "Then let me change my clothes. Apollo will not hear me unless I wear my minstrel dress."

He put on a purple robe embroidered with gold. He poured perfume on his hair, set a golden wreath upon his head, and bracelets on his arms. His lyre he held in his left hand, and struck its strings with his right hand.

The sailors were pleased to see him so richly dressed. He went to the forward part of the vessel and looked down into the sea. This was his song:

"O harp, our happy day is o'er!
On earth thy chords shall sound no more,
No more shall charm the listening maids—
My harp, we go to seek the shades.

"Ye heroes, who the flood have past,
Receive me, thus among you cast,
Although you cannot heal my grief,
Or to my sorrow bring relief.

"I die, and yet I do not fear!
The watchful gods are ever near!
You, you who slay me, soon shall know
The bitter taste of guilty woe.

"But O ye sea-nymphs, bright and fair,
My harp and I now seek your care;
Upon your mercy I depend,
Receive me as a welcome friend."

Then he sprang overboard, and sank beneath the waves. The sailors were glad to have so little trouble. He was gone, they had the prize, who could know that he had not fallen into the water by accident? Still, they rowed hard to get away from the spot.

They did not see what was going on in the water. While Arion was singing, the fish and other creatures of the sea had gathered around the ship to hear his music. When he sank down among them they came close to show their love and offer their help. One strong dolphin turned his broad back to the singer. Arion took the hint, and mounted upon the dolphin. The proud fish rose nearly to the surface of the water and carried the musician safely to land.

Arion journeyed on and soon reached Corinth.

He went with his lyre to the palace and met his friend the king.

"I have come back famous, but poor," he said. "I gained the glory and the prize, but thieves have robbed me of the gold."

When the king heard the strange history, he said, "Is power mine, and shall I not punish the guilty? Keep close until the ship comes in."

When the ship came into port, he sent for the sailors and asked them, "Where is Arion? Have you heard anything of him? He is my friend, and I am anxious to have him come back to Corinth."

They said, "We left him well and happy at Tarentum."

Then Arion stepped forward, dressed just as he was when he threw himself overboard at their command. The sailors fell on their faces. "He is a god," they said. "We killed him and he is alive." The king said, "You meant to kill him, but Heaven took care of him. Go, miserable wretches. Arion forgives you, but go to some wild land where nothing beautiful can ever give you pleasure."

CHAPTER XXI

A FIERY RUNAWAY

"**M**OTHER,**"** said young Phaeton, "is it true, as you have always told me, that the bright sun-god is my father?"

"Yes, my son," she replied. "I have told you the truth."

"But, mother," he said, "the boys do not believe me when I tell them that. They laugh at me and say I only brag. How may I know for sure that I am his son?"

"My boy," she answered, "the land of the sun lies next to ours. Go, find your father there, and he will tell you, as I do, that you belong to him."

The lad was glad to go. He traveled to India, and found there the palace of the sun. It was more splendid than anything he had ever seen. The ceilings were ivory, the doors were silver, the columns were bright with gold and precious stones. There were pictures and carvings of everything in the sky, on the earth, and under the water.

Through the open doors the boy saw the god

sitting upon his throne. His robe was purple, and around his head were rays of piercing light. The Day, the Month, the Year, and the Hours, stood near him. Spring was there, crowned with flowers; Summer, wearing a garland of ears of grain; Autumn, with his feet stained with grape-juice; and Winter, white with frost.

Phaeton was surprised and frightened at all this. The sun-god saw him, and said, "Whence do you come, and what are you seeking?"

The lad answered, "They tell me that you are my father. If it is true kindly give me some proof that will make me sure."

The sun-god said, "It is true; and the proof is that whatever you now ask I will give you!"

"Dear father," cried the youth, "for one single day let me drive your chariot."

The sun-god shook his head. "You do not know what you are asking. This makes me sorry for my promise. Not one of the gods could drive my car. The road is steep at first, the middle part is very high, and I myself am almost afraid when I see the earth and sea so far below me. The last part of the road goes down very suddenly, and there is danger of falling. The sky with its stars is forever turning around, and I must be very careful that it does not carry me away.

"Besides, there are monsters up there. You must drive by the horns of the Bull, past the Lion's jaws, near the Archer with his arrows, and between the Scorpion and the Crab. The horses are wild, their breath is fire, they pull hard upon the reins. Ask something else; do not hold me to this."

Phaeton said, "It is that one thing that I want to do. You must keep your promise, and I will take the risk."

The father was sorry, but he had to keep his word. He led his son to the golden chariot. The Dawn opened the gates of the East. The paths outside were strewn with roses. The stars began to march away, last of all the Day-star. The Hours harnessed the horses. Phaeton mounted the seat. The sun-god said, "Hold the reins tight, and do not use the whip. Follow the track the wheels have made. Do not rise too high or sink too low. The middle of the way is best and safest."

Phaeton took the reins. The horses leaped up and plunged forward. They understood that a stranger was driving them. He could not keep them in the road. They went so near the Great Bear that she was scorched with heat, and the Little Bear was frightened and tried to run away. The Serpent around the North Pole was no longer cold, but warm. He lifted up his head and began to hiss and wriggle his huge body. The plowman picked up his plow and ran.

Phaeton wished he had never undertaken to drive. He forgot the names of the horses, and could not remember whether to whip or to hold the reins tight. The Lion roared at him, the Bull bellowed, the Crab snapped its claws, the Scorpion stretched out its dreadful arms.

The frightened boy dropped the reins. The horses

went high up in the sky, then plunged down almost to the earth. The snow melted on the tops of the Alps. The clouds on the Apennines were driven away. The forests on the mountains took fire. The springs and streams were dried up. Flames caught the grain in the fields and swept away the villages. Great cities became roaring furnaces. Heat and fire and smoke covered the world.

The smoke rose up into the sky and made it black before Phaeton's eyes. The ashes were blown into his face by the winds.

The rivers began to boil. The Nile ran up into the desert and hid his head, so that it was never found until lately. The sea bubbled and steamed. Poseidon tried to look up to see what was the matter, but the heat drove him down. The ground cracked, and Pluto saw a strange and dreadful light shine into his kingdom. Earth, wild with fear, called upon Zeus for help.

"Save us, O king of the gods," she cried. "Have mercy upon us before it is too late. The grass, the trees, the cattle, and mankind are perishing. Save us quickly, O Thou, that rulest all!"

Zeus was excited and angry. He called the sun-god and all the others and said to them, "You see that this must stop. I must bring this wild drive to an end. I am sorry for the young man, but this cannot go on."

He went up into his high tower and threw a thunderbolt which struck Phaeton. His hair was already on fire. He fell, like a shooting star, into a deep river. The sun-god ran out and caught the horses and drove them into the right way. The wild ride was over.

CHAPTER XXII

WHAT A STRONG MAN DID

THERE was once a baby whom Hera, queen of the gods, hated. She sent two huge snakes to kill him in his cradle, but he sat up, caught one snake in his right hand, the other in his left hand, and choked both of them to death.

This boy was called Heracles. In the Latin language his name is changed to Hercules.

When he grew up and was very strong, Hera put him as a servant in the care of his cousin, who gave him much hard work to do.

He was sent out to kill a furious lion, which ate men and women in Nemea. Heracles shot at the beast, but the tough hide turned the arrows away. He went near, and struck the lion with a club, but he only laughed if lions ever do laugh. Then Heracles took the beast's throat in his strong hands, and finished the battle.

He threw the body over his shoulder and carried it to his cousin, who told him not to bring such things into the house, but to leave them outside. Heracles took off the lion's skin and wore it as a cloak.

HERACLES AND THE LION

He was sent to kill the Hydra. This monster had nine heads and lived in a swamp. Its breath was so poisonous that it killed many people in that neighborhood. Heracles struck off the heads with his club, but two new heads grew each time. He told his servant to build a fire, and with a lighted stick to burn each neck as soon as the head was gone, so that no new one could grow. In that way he got rid of eight heads. The ninth was immortal; it could not die. Heracles cut it off, burned the neck, and buried the head under a rock.

His next work was to clean the Augean stables. Thousands of cattle had lived in them for thirty years. Heracles had not only hands, but a head. He dug two canals, by which he let two rivers run through the stables and in one day they were clean.

His cousin's daughter wanted a girdle or belt worn by the Queen of the Amazons. These were women who were soldiers. They wore armor and fought fiercely. No men were allowed to live in their country. Heracles went to their queen and politely told her what he wanted. She said that she should be happy to please the young lady and gave him the girdle. Hera was angry because he succeeded so easily. She made herself look like an Amazon and went among the women, telling them that the stranger meant to carry off their queen. Heracles had to fight his way back to his ship, but got away safely with the belt.

He was sent to the far West to bring away the oxen of Geryon, a monster with three bodies who had a dog with two heads. Heracles reached the shore of the Atlantic Ocean, broke a mountain in two, pushed one half over into Africa, the other into Europe, and made the Straits of Gibraltar. Those mountains were afterwards called the "Pillars of Hercules." He took the oxen and drove them home to his cousin.

When Hera was married to Zeus the Earth gave her a wedding present of some golden apples. Ever since, they and the trees on which they grew had been kept by the Hesperides, daughters of King Hesperus and nieces of the giant Atlas. As usual, a dragon helped the girls keep watch. Heracles was ordered to find the golden apples and bring them back with him. After much trouble he found Atlas in Africa. The giant was holding the sky and all the stars upon his shoulders.

Heracles said to him, "You are better acquainted than I am with your nieces. Would you kindly go and ask them to give you some of their golden apples for me?"

Atlas was cross. "While I am doing that who will hold up this sky? Can you tell me?"

"Why, yes," said Heracles. "I will."

The giant grunted. Heracles stooped down and took the sky on his shoulder. The jolt caused by the change was so slight that only a few loose stars fell from their places.

Atlas stood up straight and was much pleased to be free. He went off and was gone a long time, but when he came back three golden apples were in his hands. He gave them to Heracles, took the sky again on his back, and may be found to-day, a mountain instead of a giant.

After some other labors were finished, nothing would suit his cousin but that Heracles should go to the underworld and bring up the dog with three heads, Cerberus. He could never have done that alone, but his friends the gods Athene and Hermes helped him.

They went down together, and asked King Pluto to lend them his dog. He said, "He is not a house-dog." Heracles said, "I only want to show him to a friend of mine." Pluto answered, "He is not very pretty to look at." "No," returned Heracles. "I will just take him up to my friend's palace and bring him back here again."

"You may take him" said Pluto, "but come back as soon as you can, or my people will all run away from this kingdom."

The cousin was more frightened than ever when he saw the three-headed dog following Heracles into the palace. Cerberus was sent home very soon.

In the underworld Heracles saw his friend Theseus sitting on a rock from which he could not rise. He had gone down to help a friend who wished to carry off Pluto's wife. The angry king caught them both and seated them on a rock at his palace gate, there to stay forever. The strong man took Theseus by the hand, and lifted him loose with one pull, and they went up into the light together.

When Heracles died his body was burned to ashes, but the immortal part of him was placed among the stars.

CHAPTER XXIII

A GOLDEN GIRL

SILENUS was a careless old fellow, who is often seen in pictures wearing a garland of ivy and riding on a wine cask. Dionysus, the god of vineyards, was fond of him, for the old man had been his schoolmaster. Once he wandered away, not exactly knowing what he was doing. Some countrymen found him and took him to their king, Midas. He knew Silenus and led him kindly into the palace. For ten days he treated him with the best of everything and then conducted him to Dionysus.

The god was pleased, and said to Midas, "Choose what you would like best. That shall be the reward for this kindness."

Midas said, "Grant this, that everything I touch may turn to gold."

Dionysus answered, "It shall be as you wish, but let me tell you that you have made a poor choice."

King Midas did not think so. He went away glad and proud. He broke off an oak-branch and was delighted to find in his hand a cane of solid gold. He picked up a stone; it went into his pocket a heavy lump of gold. He gathered a flower; in a moment it was a golden rose. He reached up his hand and took an apple; it changed into shining gold.

"I shall be richer than anybody," he thought. He went along singing a little song, "Rich and happy, rich and happy."

He entered his palace and said to his servants, "Bring me all the cups and dishes in the house." They obeyed. He touched the vessels, and they changed into gold.

"Of what is my dining-table made?" he asked.

The servants answered, "Of oak, your majesty."

"Follow me!" he said. They all went into the dining-hall and saw him touch the table, which was then no longer oaken, but became bright gold.

"Now bring me a splendid dinner," he ordered. "We have a proper table service, let us have something good to eat."

He sat down upon a chair; it turned to gold. His clothes had already become cloth of gold, so stiff that he could hardly move in them.

Dinner was brought in. His chair was too heavy to move, so he had another placed at the table and sat down. That seat also became gold in a moment. He took up a piece of bread; before he could break it, a change had taken place, and it was hard gold. He laid his hand on a bunch of grapes; they were so heavy that he dropped them with a clatter of gold upon the golden dish.

The king began to be frightened. "Why, at this rate I shall starve to death," he cried. "Since I can not eat, I will drink."

He seized a gold cup, full of milk which instantly turned yellower than any cream, yellow as gold. No drop could pass his lips. He was more than ever frightened.

"Miserable man that I am," he said, "I fear there is nothing but starvation before me. Bring me the princess, bring my little daughter, and let her comfort her poor rich father."

She came running in and was pleased to see so much gold. "Oh, father," she said, "where did all these pretty things come from? Gold cups and dishes, and gold grapes, and gold bread! Why, this is wonderful!"

"Come to me, darling," her father cried. "Your poor father has made a great mistake. Come and kiss me, dearest!"

She ran into his arms. She was a pretty girl, with yellow hair that some people called golden. As her father touched her, she stood still as a statue. Her rosy face changed to yellow. Her hair became an orange color. Her smile showed yellow teeth, that had once been white. Her pink arms, her lily hands, her red shoes, all were yellow. She did not move or speak, or even cry. She could not; she was a golden girl. Her father tried to lift her on his lap, but she was too heavy.

He ran as fast as he could to Dionysus.

"Oh, I was wrong," he sobbed. "You told me I had made a mistake, and it is too true. Take back your fatal gift, and oh, give me back my darling little girl!"

The god told him, "Take your child with you to the head of the river Pactolus. Wash yourself and her in the water, and you both shall be like other people again."

Midas obeyed. The little girl turned red and white again and said, "How strange! See, father, how the sands in the river-bed sparkle! They look like gold!"

They were gold, but she was flesh again. Midas had lost his strange power, but he was much happier. Ever afterwards the sands of Pactolus were golden.

Midas made another mistake. He said that the god Pan could make better music than the god Apollo. From that time his ears began to grow long and hairy.

To hide them he put on a large turban, such as the Turks now wear. But his barber could not help seeing them. The hair-dresser did not dare to tell his wife, but he could not keep such a secret. He went out by the river bank, dug a hole, whispered into it, "King Midas has ass's ears!" and filled up the hole again.

Soon a crop of reeds sprang up there, and as the wind blew through them, the people passing by heard them whisper,

"King
Midas
has
ass's
ears!"

CHAPTER XXIV

HOW DEATH WAS CONQUERED

APOLLO had a son Æsculapius, whom he taught to be so good a doctor that it was said he could even bring the dead back to life. Pluto was displeased at this, for it was taking away his rights, so he asked Zeus to throw a thunderbolt at the doctor. That killed him. Nobody could bring him back to life, and Apollo was very angry. He went to Mount Ætna, where the Cyclopes worked at making thunderbolts for the king of heaven. These were an entirely different family from those Cyclopes whom Ulysses afterwards met in his wanderings. There were only three of these, and they were industrious blacksmiths, who were kept busy forging bolts for Zeus. Their shop was under the mountain, and from it came the smoke and fire of the volcano.

Apollo shot his arrows at them and greatly annoyed them, but he could not kill them. They cried out to Zeus and asked him to command Apollo not to shoot at them any more. Zeus called the sun-god and said, "You must stop annoying my faithful servants. They are not to blame. They only made the thunderbolts; I cast them where I please. You must arrange your affairs in the sun for a year's absence. During that time you must be servant to a mortal on the earth. That shall be your punishment."

"Very well," said Apollo. "Your will is my law. I have a friend who is king of Thessaly and keeps a great many sheep. I should like to be shepherd for him during that year."

It was so ordered. Apollo went, a fine young man, to Admetus, king of Thessaly, and was given charge of his sheep. He took good care of them, and they seemed very happy. He made the fields bright, the river sparkled when he stood on its banks, and when he was in the palace it was full of sunshine.

Admetus was himself a young man and he was in love with Alcestis. She was the daughter of a king, who said to young men, "Do you see my daughter Alcestis? Should you like to marry her? You may, on one condition. Come for her in a chariot; but understand, it must be drawn, not by horses, or mules, or oxen, but by lions and boars. When will you come for her—next week?"

Then the young men would go away disappointed and angry. Admetus was one of them. He told his shepherd about this foolish saying of the old king. "Is that all?" said the bright shepherd. "That can be easily settled."

He went out and caught two lions and two boars and tamed them, for what creature could disobey him? He harnessed them to the chariot of Admetus and said, "There is your team. Drive over and get your bride and bring her home, and let us all be happy together."

The team did not pull very fast at first. The lions wanted to eat the boars, and the boars tried to tear the lions with their tusks. But after a while they became used to each other, and went off roaring and grunting in fine style.

When they reached the home of Alcestis her father was surprised, but kept his promise. She mounted the chariot with Admetus, and such a wedding procession as followed them to the temple was never before known. All the countryside turned out to see the wonderful team of wild beasts.

Admetus and Alcestis were very happy, for they loved each other dearly. But the young husband fell sick and was near death. Apollo could not cure him, but went to the Fates, whom he knew, and begged them to spare the young king. They promised on one condition,—that someone else should agree to die in his stead. Admetus thought he could easily find such a friend. He went for his soldiers who had fought for him, but they said, "Oh, no! It is one thing to die in the excitement of battle, giving and taking fatal blows, but quite another to die in cold blood for somebody else."

Then he sent for old servants who had but a little while to live; but they said, "Oh, no! Life is dear to us as to anybody. Each man must stand in his own place. When our turn comes we must go, but not before."

A friend said, "Why not ask your father or your mother? They love you, and they have not long to live. One of them will surely die in your place."

But they said, "Oh, no! Dear son, we love you, but how can we give up our lives, even for your sake?"

The young king was all the time growing worse. It was plain that he had not long to live. Alcestis said, "O cruel Fates, that have no mercy on loving hearts, you mean to part us! Have, then, your will! Since I must lose my husband by his death or my own, let it be mine. He shall live and see the bright sunshine and the sweet flowers and the pleasant faces of friends. I must wander in the gloomy fields of the underworld among the pale ghosts that dwell there."

Admetus was not willing that his darling should die, but the Fates would not be trifled with. He grew better but his wife was faint and pale, and near the end of life.

Just then Heracles came by and heard the sad story.

"I will save her," he said.

He stood outside the door of her room. Death came to claim his own—himself a monster so frightful that none could look on him and live. In the dark, Heracles caught him in his strong arms. They wrestled and struggled for a long while, until Death called out, "Spare me, Heracles. The queen is yours. Keep her and let me go." The hero loosed his hold, and Death went away. Heracles went into the queen's room and kissed her thin hand and said, "He has gone. You are to stay with us. Smile and get well, and be happy with your husband."

CHAPTER XXV

THE SHEPHERD
PRINCE OF TROY

PRIAM, king of Troy, lived in a splendid city called Ilion, with many sons and daughters around him. One of the sons, named Paris, had a strange history. He was only a few days old when his mother dreamed that he caught up a blazing torch and ran through the city, setting it on fire. The king asked an oracle what that dream meant. He was told that it would all come true. Priam ordered that the child should be taken to Mount Ida, on the eastern side of the kingdom, and left there to die.

Some shepherds found the boy and brought him up as their son. He was strong and bold and liked to fight, to wrestle, and to run with the other young shepherds. They called him Alexander, which means, "Defender of men."

When everybody was afraid to race or fight with him, he was made umpire of their games. He always gave just decisions, and even the gods knew that he was fair and honest.

At a feast on Olympus the goddess of Discord threw on the table a golden apple, marked, "For the most beautiful." Hera said, "That is for me. Who is so beautiful as the queen of heaven?"

But Athene stretched out her hand and said, "No, it is for me. Who can equal me in the beauty of wisdom?"

Then Aphrodite rose up and said, "It is for me. Gods and men know that I am most beautiful."

There was a bitter quarrel, until some one said, "Let us go to the shepherd of Mount Ida; he will decide rightly." It was agreed, and Paris saw all heaven coming to him on the mountain-side. Among so much beauty and power the shepherd found it hard to choose. The goddesses made him fine promises.

Hera said, "Give me the prize, and I will make you the most powerful king in the world."

Athene said, "None shall be like you for wisdom if you give me the apple."

Aphrodite smiled on the youth and said, "Give it to me, and you shall have for a wife the most beautiful woman in the world."

He gave her the golden apple, and from that moment Hera and Athene hated him and his family.

King Priam knew nothing of all this. He intended to have a contest among the young princes, his neighbors, and the prize was to be the finest bull upon Mount Ida. Officers looking for such an animal found it in the herd of Paris.

THE DECISION OF PARIS

"Shepherd," they said, "the king has need of this beast."

"Why does he want him?" inquired Paris. The officers answered, "To be the prize of the royal games. How much is he worth?"

Paris replied, "He is not for sale." When the officers urged him he said, "You can not have the bull unless I may enter the games and have a chance to win the prize."

When this was told the king he said, "Let the bold shepherd come." Paris went to Troy, and in the games conquered everybody except Hector, the king's oldest son. The younger man was afraid of this great hero, so he dropped his sword and ran for his life.

When Paris reached the temple of Zeus he went in and was safe. Nobody would dare to harm him in that holy place.

Cassandra, his sister, was a prophetess in that temple. She cried out that this was not a shepherd, but the king's son; that his name was not Alexander, but Paris; and that Hector was his brother. They all went to the palace, and Priam was glad to see again his child whom he had sent away to die. He welcomed the youth to his royal home, and gave him every right of a king's son.

Paris as a prince was not so happy as he had been when a shepherd. He lived in the city instead of on the mountain, and had nothing to do but amuse himself.

His clothes were very fine and set off his handsome face and figure. But he grew tired of home and friends.

"Father," he said to Priam, "let me go abroad and see something of the world."

The king thought well of the plan, so he gave Paris money, and sent him to travel with several gay young men like himself. They journeyed from island to island, and came at last to Sparta where Menelaus was king. He welcomed the young travelers and was very kind to them. In a few days he said to his guests, "I must go to Crete on important business. Excuse me for leaving you, but my queen will do all she can to make you comfortable while I am gone."

That queen was named Helen and was the most beautiful woman in the world. When she was a girl many princes had asked her in marriage, but she did not care for any of them.

Her father said to these princes, "I can give her to only one. You must not quarrel about her. Let each man promise to be satisfied when she has made her choice, and to defend her husband against all enemies."

They promised, and she choose Menelaus, king of Sparta, and went with him to his home.

They had lived happily for some years when Paris came. He was a prince, rich, fair to see, and with very pleasant manners. Helen was young and weak. She forgot her duty, fell in love with Paris, and went with him to Troy.

Aphrodite had kept her promise. Paris had the

most beautiful wife in the world. But sorrow, misery, and death followed, as they are sure to follow selfishness and deceit. Menelaus called all the princes of Greece and of the islands to help him get back Helen. They raised a large army and sailed against Troy. This was the beginning of the Trojan war, which lasted for ten years.

CHAPTER XXVI

THE TROJAN WAR

WHEN Paris had carried off Helen to Troy, her husband Menelaus called on the Greek leaders to help him bring her back. That meant war, and some were very unwilling to risk their lives and the lives of their soldiers in such a cause. One named Odysseus, whom we will call by his Latin name, Ulysses, pretended to be insane. He yoked up a donkey and a cow to the plow, and sowed salt in his field. The messenger who had been sent to him placed the little son of Ulysses before the plow. Of course the father turned his strange team aside and could no longer pretend to be out of his mind.

He persuaded several to go with him to the war, among them Achilles. The mother of this young man was unwilling to have him fight against Troy, so she dressed him like a girl and placed him among the daughters of a friendly king. Ulysses heard of this and put on the clothes of a traveling merchant. He went to the palace with rings and bracelets and belts, and two or three good swords. The girls came out to see these treasures and were pleased with the jewelry. One among them did not look at the rings and ornaments, but lifted the swords and tried their weight.

Ulysses said, "Young man, your dress is that of a girl, but your eye is that of a man. You are Achilles, and you must go with me to Ilion and to battle."

Two years were spent in collecting ships and men. The entire company met at Aulis, ready to sail together. But the winds were contrary, and no vessel could leave the port. A deadly sickness broke out among the men. It was found that one of the chiefs had hunted and killed a stag sacred to Artemis, who was very angry. The fortune-teller, or soothsayer, who was with the company, said that the goddess demanded the sacrifice of Iphigenia, the daughter of the chief.

The maiden was sent for and came, not knowing what was to be done. An altar had been built. She was bound and placed upon it, while the leaders stood waiting to see her die. The priest raised the knife to strike, but a thick cloud came down and hid the altar, and the girl was gone. The goddess carried her to Tauris and made her a priestess in the temple there.

The sickness passed away. The wind blew strongly out of the port. The fleet sailed and soon reached the coast of Troy. War began at once and lasted for nine years without seeming any nearer an end.

A quarrel arose between Achilles and Agamemnon, the king whose daughter was to have been sacrificed at Aulis. Achilles said he would fight no more, but would go home to Greece.

The gods and goddesses took a deep interest in the case. Hera and Athene were angry at Paris and the Trojans, but Aphrodite was friendly to them. Ares took her side, but Poseidon helped the Greeks.

Fighting went on more fiercely than ever. The Trojans won victory after victory, and the Greeks were driven to their ships. The enemy followed and were about to burn the vessels, when Poseidon went among the Greeks as a soothsayer and gave them new courage. Ajax the Greek met Hector of Troy, who darted his lance, which struck but did no harm. Then Ajax took a huge stone and threw it with all his might. It fell on Hector like a falling mountain, and he sank to the ground hurt and stunned. Zeus sent Apollo to cure him, and he soon was busy again in the fight.

The battle went against the Greeks. Some chiefs were wounded, others were killed. Once more the Trojans reached the ships and were preparing to burn them.

A dear friend of Achilles, named Patroclus, went to the hero and said, "Oh, my friend! if you will not come and help us, lend me your armor and your soldiers, that I may drive away these enemies before they destroy all our ships."

Achilles said, "Take my armor and my men and drive away our foes, but do not try to follow them without my help."

The Trojans thought they saw the great Achilles with his troops coming against them. They fled, and Patroclus followed, driving them like sheep, until he met Hector. These two fought, and Patroclus fell. Then Hector took from him the armor of Achilles and put it on.

When Achilles heard that his friend was dead he started up and said, "I will go out and fight with Hector this very day."

His mother said, "Remember, you have no armor. Wait until to-morrow, and you shall have a suit better than the first."

She hastened to Hephæstus, who made the armor, and at the dawn of day it lay at the feet of Achilles. He went into the battle and drove the Trojans inside the wall of their city.

Only Hector stood outside waiting to meet him, but when he saw Achilles coming he turned and ran. Achilles followed him three times around the city; then Hector stood and fought. The spear of Achilles pierced him, and he fell.

Achilles striped the armor from the body, tied Hector's feet behind his chariot, and drove around the city, dragging the dead hero through the dust. The Trojans stood weeping on the walls, among them the father and mother and wife of Hector, lamenting at the dreadful sight.

The Greeks took the body of Patroclus and burned it with many honors, but Hector's corpse lay out upon the plain. Priam, his father and king of Troy, heaped a litter full of gold and rich dresses and other costly gifts. The gods helped him and his servants to carry it to the tent of Achilles as a ransom for the corpse of Hector. It was accepted, and the weeping company carried back those poor remains to the city and gave them the highest funeral honors.

CHAPTER XXVII

THE WOODEN HORSE

T HE brave Hector was dead, but other friends went to the help of Troy. One of these was Penthesilea, queen and leader of the Amazons. These were women who were brave fighters, and who did not permit any men to live in their country. The queen met death at the hands of Achilles, who was very sorry afterwards.

When Achilles was a child his mother had dipped him in the river Styx, and the heel by which she had held him was the only spot where he could be hurt.

During the war with Troy he had seen and loved Priam's daughter, Polyxena. He told the Trojans that if she would marry him, he would try to make peace between them and the Greeks. While the matter was being talked over in the temple of Apollo, Paris, with a poisoned arrow, shot Achilles in the heel. He died; and Ajax and Ulysses carried back his body to the ships. The shining armor was given to Ulysses.

The Trojans had a statue of Athene, which was said to have fallen from heaven. It was called the

Palladium, and they believe that while it was safe among them their city could never be taken. Ulysses and a friend went into the city one night, entered the temple, took the statue, and carried it to the Greek ships.

Even then the city stood unconquered. Ulysses thought of a plan by which it might be captured. Some of the ships were taken away and hidden behind an island. Many men worked at building a large wooden horse, which they said was to be offered to Athene. It was hollow, and a number of soldiers crept into it, after which it was closed up and left standing in the camp.

The rest of the Greeks went on board their ships and rowed away. The Trojans thought their enemies were gone forever. So they came out of their city and walked about, glad to be free. They went to the deserted camp of the Greeks, and picked up old swords and broken helmets and other things that had been left on the ground.

Everybody wondered at the huge horse standing there. "What can be the use of that?" said some. Others said, "Let us take it into the city and put it in some temple." Still others declared that it would be far better not to touch it, but to leave it entirely alone.

Laocoön was a priest of the temple of Poseidon. He advised them to be very careful. "Have you not already suffered enough from the fraud of our enemies? As for me, I fear the Greeks even when they bring gifts."

He threw his spear at the horse's side. A sound like a groan followed the blow. The people were about to break and burn the horse when a crowd of men were seen dragging along a frightened Greek. His name was Sinon, and it was part of the plan that he should remain in the camp, so that he might be captured by the Trojans.

The leaders asked him why he was there and what was the meaning of this horse. He told them that Ulysses hated him, and had left him on shore when the rest of the Greeks went away. The horse, he said, was an offering to Athene. It had been made very large so that it might not be carried into the city. "Our prophet told us," he added, "that if the Trojans ever took it they would surely conquer us."

While the people were wondering how they could get the horse into the city, two large snakes came up out of the sea. They went straight to the place where Laocoön's two sons were standing together, and began to twine around them. The father ran to help his boys, but the serpents wrapped themselves around him also. The helpless Trojans stood by and saw the priest and his children crushed and strangled in those dreadful folds.

The people now thought that the horse must truly be sacred, and with much labor, yet rejoicing, carried it into the city. At night Sinon, the Greek, opened the horse and let out the soldiers. He also opened the gates of the city to the other Greeks, who had come silently back.

The Trojans had gone happily to sleep, thinking it needless to keep a watch, because no enemy was near.

They were wakened by the light of a great fire. Their temples were in flames. They rushed into the streets astonished and frightened. Greek soldiers met them at their doors and showed them no mercy.

The old king Priam put on his armor that he might fight; but the queen, Hecuba, persuaded him to go with her to the temple of Zeus and pray for help. While they were kneeling at the altar their youngest son rushed in and fell dead at their feet. After him came the son of Achilles, who had wounded him. Priam threw his spear at this fierce enemy, but the young man struck him down beside his son.

Ilion, or Troy, was entirely destroyed. Many of the people were killed. Many more, with the old queen and her daughter, were carried away as captives.

Paris was among the dead. Menelaus found his wife Helen, who had caused all this trouble and misery, and they went back to Sparta, their old home. The Greek leaders gathered their men who were left, and set sail for the land they had not seen for ten long years. The Trojan war was over, and Troy was no more.

CHAPTER XXVIII

THE GIANT'S CAVE

WHEN the Trojan war was ended, Ulysses called together his men, and with several vessels sailed for Ithaca and home. Many strange things were to happen to him before he saw his wife and son.

A storm drove the little fleet to the land of the Lotus-eaters. The lotus is a water plant, and the people ate the yellow buds. Then they never wished to live anywhere else, or even to see any other country. It was so with every one who ate the lotus.

Three friends of Ulysses went up the hill, found the people, and ate some of the buds. They did not go back to the ship. Others were sent to bring them, but they said, "We do not wish to go home. We are at home here in this lovely land." The other sailors dragged them to the ship and kept them tied until they were far out at sea.

The ships touched at an island, where they anchored. Ulysses took one vessel and went ashore to get something for his men to eat. The sailors carried a large skin of wine, as a present to the king.

They saw nobody, but found a cave and went in. There were lambs and young goats in pens, piles of cheeses, bowls of milk; everything to show that somebody carried on a good dairy business.

While they were looking around they heard the patter of many feet, and a large flock of sheep and goats began to come into the cave. The men hid themselves until they should see what the master was like.

They were not pleased with the sight. He was a huge giant, very strong and very ugly. He had one large, round eye in the middle of his forehead. For that reason he was called a "Cyclops," which means "round eye." A tribe of such giants lived in the caves of that island.

This Cyclops was named Polyphemus. When the flock was all in, he shut the opening of the cave with a very large stone, lighted a fire, milked his sheep and goats, put aside some of the milk to be made into cheese, and drank the rest.

Then he had time to look around the cave and see his visitors. In a frightful, roaring voice he asked, "Who are you, and where do you come from?"

"Great sir," replied Ulysses, "we are men of Ithaca, who have fought in the Trojan war and gained much glory. We are now going home, and ask you, in the name of the gods, to give us food and shelter to-night, and send us safely away in the morning."

The giant did not speak, but stretched out his

hand and caught two of the men, knocked their heads against the wall, and quickly ate them. Then he threw himself down on the floor and went to sleep.

Ulysses could have killed him with his sword, but how then would he and his companions escape? They could never roll away that stone. There was no help for it; they had to wait until the morning.

When the morning came it brought no light to that dark cave. The giant took two more Greeks and ate them for breakfast. Then he opened the cave, drove out his flock, and rolled the heavy stone into its place again. The men were prisoners.

They kept up the fire, which gave them light to look around. They found a large stick,—the trunk of a tree, in fact,—which the giant had used as a cane or walking-stick. Ulysses told his men to sharpen it with their swords to a point, and to harden that in the fire. He chose four of the bravest sailors to act with him when the time came.

At night the Cyclops returned, shut his cave tight, milked his flocks, and made a hearty supper of two more Greeks. Then Ulysses came forward with a bowl he had filled with wine. "Drink, master," he said. "Your slaves offer you wine." The giant tasted, and drank it all. "More," he said. They filled the bowl again and again until the skin was empty.

Polyphemus had never felt so gay in all his life. He laughed, he sang in a voice that shook the mountain, he joked with his prisoners.

IN THE GIANT'S CAVE

"What is your name?" he asked Ulysses. "I am called No-man," was the answer. "Well, No-man, you are a fine little fellow. That wine you gave me was better than milk. I am sorry it is all gone. Rest easy, and be happy, No-man. I shall eat you the last of all."

He was soon fast asleep. Ulysses told his four men to take the stake, and hold the point in the fire until it was a hot coal, then to lift it and plunge it into the monster's one eye. Ulysses had ordered them to turn it around, and they ground it in well.

The blinded monster roared with pain and rage and stumbled about the cave, trying to find his enemies. The fire was still burning, and they could see how to keep out of his way. Then he called on his friends, the other Cyclopes who lived on the island, and they came running.

"What is it, brother?" they shouted. "Why do you call and cry so loudly?"

"Oh!" he said, "I die, and No-man kills me."

They answered, "If it is no man, it must be the gods who are punishing you. Try to be patient." Then they went away home.

In the morning the Cyclops rolled away the stone to let his flock out, but stood at the mouth of the cave. Ulysses had told his men to harness the biggest sheep, three abreast, with willow twigs which the giant had gathered for making baskets. Under each middle sheep a Greek hid himself, holding fast to the wool. The Cyclops felt the sides and back of every sheep, to be sure that no Greek was riding them, but never thought of feeling underneath.

So all got out safe, Ulysses last, and drove part of the flocks down to the ship. Their friends gladly took on board the men and the sheep. When they were some distance from the shore, Ulysses called out, "Cyclops, I am Ulysses, and I am also No-man." The giant threw rocks in the direction of the voice, but the sailors rowed away, and reached the other ships.

CHAPTER XXIX

THE ENCHANTED ISLAND

ULYSSES and his crew arrived at another island, and lived for two or three days upon its shores. Then Ulysses climbed a hill and saw in the center of the isle a palace almost hidden in trees.

Much trouble had made him careful. He went down to his men and said, "I see in the distance a noble house, but none of us can tell what creatures may live there. We will divide into two parties. I shall stay with one half on the shore near our vessels; the other half will go forward and find out what land this is and what welcome we may hope for."

There were forty-four of the crew, besides Ulysses and his lieutenant. The latter with twenty-two men went up into the island. They saw the palace among the trees, a stately building, with smoke rising from the kitchen chimneys. That made them glad, for they were hungry.

As they drew near the house a number of wild beasts came running toward them. There were lions, tigers, wolves, and other fierce creatures. The sailors were brave men, and they prepared to fight. But these creatures, though they roared and howled, did no harm. In fact, they seemed to be very friendly.

The companions of Ulysses went on and reached the portico of the house. The doors were open, and they heard the sound of a loom and of voices singing. Even royal ladies wove in those days, and this seemed like a safe and comfortable house. But the lieutenant thought it best to be careful. He said to the men, "Somebody must watch. Go in and see what is there. I will wait behind this pillar until you come and tell me that all is well."

The crew entered the wide doors. A smiling lady, attended by her maidens, met them and gave them welcome.

"Come freely in," she said. "I see by your looks that you are mariners who have sailed far and suffered much. This is a house of rest for such. My maids will show you to the dining-hall, where you can feast at your ease."

The poor sailors were very happy to be so well received. They were placed on couches, and food and wine were brought to them. They ate and drank heartily and were full of joy.

Then the lady said sharply, "Look at me!" They lifted up their eyes, a little heavy with feasting, and saw her looking angrily at them. In her hand she held a long and slender rod.

"You were beasts when you came," she said, "and

now you shall be beasts forever. Go to the sty and join your proper companions."

She struck every one of the men a sharp blow with her rod. Each saw his companions changed, in an instant, into swine. All found themselves wallowing and grunting on the floor. The girls took sticks and drove these creatures out of the palace and into the pigpen.

There, with many more of their kind, they were fed on acorns and other swinish food.

The lieutenant ran down to the ship and told the dreadful story. Ulysses said, "This calls for my help. Stay here, all of you. I will go alone."

On the way he met the god Hermes, who told him that this was the enchanted island of Circe, a powerful witch, who delighted in trapping men and changing them into beasts. The lions, tigers, bears, and wolves had once been human, but the cup and rod of Circe had made them what they now were.

"Do not risk yourself in that palace," said Hermes. "Sail away with the men you have left and find some safer land than this."

"Run away and leave my poor companions in a pigsty?" cried Ulysses. "Never! I will set them free or share their fate."

"Very well," said Hermes. "I like to see a man stand by his friends. I will help you."

He plucked a flower and gave it to Ulysses. "That is a moly," he said, "and it is a charm against all kinds of magic. Keep it in your hand and smell it often."

Ulysses went to the palace. Circe came to meet him and said with smiles, "This is the king! I know you by your noble bearing. This must be the great Ulysses. You are welcome to my poor house. It is yours more than it is mine."

"Madam," he said, "where are my friends? They came here to-day, and I am now seeking them. I trust they have not met with any harm."

"Any harm!" she answered. "No harm could touch them in my palace. Come in and eat and drink. My maidens will lead you then to your friends, and you can all be happy together."

Ulysses followed her and ate and drank but kept the moly in his hand and smelled it often.

At last, the witch struck him with her rod. "Too long," she said, "too long you keep that human shape, of which you are not worthy. Go, join your companions in the sty, and wallow with them there."

Ulysses leaped from the couch and drew his sword.

"No!" he cried. "Wicked witch, whom gods hate and men fear, you have met your master. Give me back my friends in their natural shapes, or you shall die."

He caught her by the hair and raised her glittering blade.

"Spare me," she said, "and I will do all your bidding. You are wise and brave, fit to be my master. I will obey you."

The pigs were brought from the sty. Circe used some magic words and touched them with her rod. They stood up as sailors, just as they had been. Then the other men were called up from the shore, and all feasted together. But Ulysses always kept the moly with him, and watched that Circe should not deceive him.

CHAPTER XXX

DANGERS OF THE SEA

BEFORE Ulysses and his men reached Circe's island, they had stopped at the country where Æolus lived. He had charge of the winds, and could send out gentle breezes or wild storms as he chose. He was glad to see Ulysses and gave him a leather bag tied with a silver string. In it all the hindering and dangerous winds were safely shut up. The fair and favoring winds were free to blow the ships along to their home country.

Ulysses steered the boat for nine days and then, tired out, lay down to sleep. The foolish sailors had often looked at the strange bag and wondered what it held. They thought that it must be gold, and that they ought to have their share. They untied the string to get some of the money, but the angry winds rushed out, the ships were caught in a fierce storm, and were blown back to the island of Æolus. He was angry and would not help them again, so they had to row all the way, until they came to the enchanted island.

After spending some time in the palace of Circe, they set out once more upon their voyage. Circe gave them good advice and told them how to escape the Sirens. These creatures looked like beautiful women. They sat on dangerous rocks in the sea and sang so sweetly that every sailor who heard them was bewitched and let his boat drift until it was dashed among the rocks, and he was lost.

Circe told Ulysses to fill the ears of his men with wax so that they could not hear, and to have himself bound tight to the mast, with orders that no one should untie him until they had safely passed the island of the Sirens. This was done. As they drew near the place, Ulysses could hear the sweetest music. "Oh!" he cried, "home and joy are in those sounds. Row in that direction; we shall find our dear ones there, and every delight we have ever known or hoped for."

The rowers only stared at him. They heard nothing.

"Slaves!" he shouted. "Am not I your master? Do as I bid you! Dogs that you are, do you dare to disobey me? If you will not row toward those divine voices, at least unbind me and let me swim to them."

Two men rose up and went toward him. He thought they would untie him and said to them, "Brave fellows, thank you, thank you!" But they only took more cords and bound him tighter. He was furious and called them many hard names, but they rowed on. The voices of the Sirens died away. The danger was over, the isle had been safely passed. Ulysses was ashamed of his folly. "You did well to bind me," he said to his men. "Without that I should have gone to my death."

There were other dangers ahead. The ships had to pass between Scylla and Charybdis. Scylla had once been a pretty girl, but Circe changed her into a horrid monster. She lived in a cave on the side of a cliff. The water passage below was very narrow, and she stretched down her six long necks, each with a head at the end, and with her mouths caught six sailors from every ship that passed within her reach.

On the other side of the strait was the whirlpool Charybdis. Three times every day the water rushed into a deep gulf and was cast out again. If the tide, while going in, caught a vessel, nothing could save her. She must certainly be wrecked.

Ulysses heard the roar of the whirlpool, and keeping far away from it, sailed close to the cliff where Scylla lived. She darted out her six heads, laid hold of six men with her teeth, and dragged them up on the rock to eat them. Nobody could help them. They were gone forever.

The wanderers came next to the island where the cattle of the sun pastured. Ulysses gave strict orders that the beasts should not be touched. But contrary winds kept the ship there for a month. All the food was eaten. The sailors caught birds and fish, but still were very hungry. One day, when Ulysses was absent, they killed some of the sacred cows and ate the flesh, first offering part of it in a sacrifice to the sun-god.

When Ulysses came back, he was frightened to see the skins of the cows creeping along the ground, while large joints of meat were roasting before the fire and mooing as they cooked.

The wind changed, and the wanderers left that dreadful shore. Soon a great storm arose. Lightning struck the mast and killed the pilot. The vessel was broken to pieces, and the crew sank in the waters. The keel and mast of the ship floated side by side. Ulysses tied them together with ropes and made a raft. On this he floated alone to an island where he found a friend and help.

CHAPTER XXXI

A FRIENDLY LAND

IT was the island of Calypso upon which Ulysses had been cast. She was a sea-nymph, or goddess of the sea. She treated the stranger well, and he remained on the island for some time, but at last he built for himself a raft, took some food on board, and pushed off into the broad sea.

After floating for many days his raft was broken in a storm, but he reached land at the mouth of a gentle river. Near the shore was a wood, where he heaped leaves together and lay down to sleep, very tired but very glad to be safe on dry ground.

The land was called Scheria, and the people living there were happy and peaceful. They had neither swords nor bows. Their chief business and great delight was sailing ships.

That very night, while Ulysses was sleeping under the trees, the king's daughter had a dream. Athene appeared to her and said, "My child, do you remember that your wedding day will soon be here? The family should all be dressed in clean white robes that will

THE WRECKED ULYSSES

shine like silver. Go to-morrow with your maidens, and see that every garment of the household is well and carefully washed, to be ready for the great occasion."

The princess was named Nausicaa. In the morning she asked her father and mother if they did not think it was time to have the family washing done. They said, "Yes," and the king ordered the chariot to be got ready and loaded with clothes. A good supply of food was also put in, and the princess took the driver's seat and handled the reins. The maidens followed on foot and the procession moved toward the river.

When the clothes were washed and spread out to dry, the girls ate their dinner and began to play ball. The ball rolled into the river; whereupon the maidens screamed, and Ulysses awoke.

He came out of the woods, a wretched object. His hair and beard were long and tangled, his eyes were wild with hunger, his clothes were few and miserable. When the maidens saw him, they ran away frightened. But the king's daughter stood still, for she was of royal blood and not a coward.

Ulysses broke off a leafy branch from a tree, and held it before him to hide his raggedness. He told the princess that he was a shipwrecked stranger and asked her help. She called back her maidens and gave him food and some of her brother's clothes, which had been in the chariot. Then she drove home, telling him to follow at a little distance.

On the way Athene met him, gave him some advice, and hid him in a cloud that he might go unseen through the city. He saw the harbor, the ships, the houses, and the people, yet reached the palace unnoticed. Its doors were gold, its doorposts of silver. Near it was a garden full of delicious fruits and flowers. Everything outside the house was charming, as everything within was peaceful. The king, his family, and the great men, were sitting at supper. The cloud melted away, and they saw Ulysses, standing in the middle of the hall. He went to the queen, knelt before her, and asked her kind help to reach his native country. Then he took a seat by the fire, as beggars did in those days.

The king said to his son, "It would be like a prince to give the stranger your place." The youth rose up, took Ulysses by the hand and led him to a seat, where he ate and drank among the nobles of the land.

After the feast, when the others had gone away to their homes, he told the king and queen his story. They promised him a ship which should take him to his own kingdom.

The next day the chief men agreed with the king that the stranger should be kindly sent home. A ship and its rowers were chosen, and all went to the palace for a farewell feast. Afterwards in the arena, the young men held games, with running, wrestling, and other sports. They invited Ulysses to take part, but he asked to be excused.

One of the young men said, "Why do you trouble the stranger? He is old, his joints are stiff, he is not able to do what we can do!"

Ulysses found a quoit, or weight, much heavier

than had yet been thrown, and sent it whirling through the air. It fell far beyond the best throw made by any of the young men.

They went back to the hall, and a blind bard, or minstrel, was led in. He sang about the wooden horse and the fall of Troy. The company was pleased, but it brought back old times to the memory of Ulysses, and his eyes were filled with tears.

The king said, "Noble stranger, you weep! Why does the song make you sorrowful? Did you lose at Troy a father, a brother or a dear friend?"

Ulysses stood up and said, "I was at Troy. The wooden horse was made by my advice. I fought beside the Greek heroes and saw many of them fall. I weep for the days and men that are no more."

He told them all his story. They gave him rich presents and sent him home. When the ship reached the port he was asleep. The sailors did not waken him, but carried him and his chests of presents to the shore; then they sailed away to their own land.

CHAPTER XXXII

THE WANDERER'S RETURN

W HEN Ulysses awoke he did not know where he was. But the friendly Athene came as usual and told him many things. He had been gone for twenty years, and most people thought he must be dead. A hundred princes had visited his wife, Penelope, asking her to marry them. As she could not marry all, and did not wish to marry any, they had agreed among themselves to stay at her palace until she made up her mind to choose one of them. Then the rest would go away.

Penelope believed that her husband was alive. To put off these troublesome suitors she said, "When my maidens and I have finished this piece of embroidery, I will say who shall be my husband."

It was a very large cloth, and although the girls worked hard, it was never near being done. Penelope and her maidens picked out at night all the stitches they had put in by day.

Athene made Ulysses look like a beggar, and he went up to the palace. Nobody noticed him except the swineherd, who gave him some food and rest.

Telemachus, the son of Ulysses, came in, and Athene changed the beggar back to his real self. The young man did not know his father, but they soon became acquainted. They planned to get rid of the troublesome suitors. The son was to go in as usual, and the father would come as a beggar, who would tell stories to pay for his dinner.

So it was done. As Ulysses went through the courtyard, an old dog lifted his head, crawled forward, and licked the stranger's feet. He remembered his master, with whom he had so often hunted twenty years before.

The princes were in high glee. They ate and drank and joked, and one of them struck the beggar with a stool. They declared that they would not be put off any longer. Penelope must decide that day. Her son said they were right, but a trial of skill must first be held. Each must shoot with a bow, and he whose arrow went through twelve rings set in a row should have the prize. An old bow belonging to Ulysses was brought into the hall, with plenty of arrows. All other weapons were taken away.

Telemachus tried to bend the bow so as to string it, but could not. Prince after prince tried in vain. The beggar said, "Let me try. Believe me, poor as I am now, I was a soldier once, and these old arms may still have some strength."

The suitors were angry, but Telemachus said it could do no harm to let the old man try. Ulysses took the bow, bent it, and fastened the cord. He picked up an arrow, fitted it to the string, and sent it darting through the twelve rings.

The suitors were astonished. Ulysses shouted, "My son, my swineherd, every friend of mine, to my side! I am Ulysses; I am the master here."

Telemachus and the servants hurried for arms, which they had hidden not far away. They stood beside Ulysses, and the princes saw themselves ensnared. They rushed to the doors, but found them fastened. Then they drew together at one end of the hall, panting like wild beasts that are caught in a trap. They had nothing to fight with, not even a dagger.

"We are defeated," they said. "Open your doors, and give us liberty to go to our homes. We will trouble you no more."

"No!" said Ulysses, who was no longer a beggar, but stood like a king before them. "No! You will trouble me no more! I shall take care of that. Here in my palace you have lived and feasted, eating my substance, abusing my servants, making my wife miserable with your hated offers. You thought me dead, but I live and have come to my own again. Dear wife and son, I am your protector. See, I drive these enemies before me as the stormwind drives withered leaves!"

PART II
HISTORICAL STORIES

CHAPTER XXXIII

THE SPLENDID CITY

A THENS is a very old city. Cecrops, who came from Egypt, is said to have founded it. The fables tell us that he was half man and half dragon, and though we know this is not true it may be true that there was a man named Cecrops and that he did begin to build the city. At first it was called after him, Cecropia, but the people were so fond of the goddess Athene that its name was changed to Athens.

The fables say that Poseidon, the god of the sea, wanted the men of the city to worship him. So he struck the rock, and a beautiful horse appeared. Then Athene struck the ground, and an olive tree sprung up. Cecrops said, "O goddess, your gift is best! The city will always honor and worship you."

Athens stands in the central plan of Attica, three miles back from the sea. All around the plain are mountains except for the south, which is open to the sea.

There are four hills in the city, the Acropolis, the Areopagus, the Pynx, and the Museum. The Acropolis is the highest, rising one hundred and fifty feet above the plain. It is very steep on every side except the west, which has a slope not easy to climb. The flat top is about one thousand feet long and five hundred feet broad.

West from the Acropolis stands the Areopagus, or the Hill of Mars, where the courts of justice were held. Sixteen steps cut in the rock lead up from the market place to the top, where the Council used to meet. Around three sides of the top, benches are cut out of the solid rock. The fourth side looks to the south and is open. On the west side is a raised block on which the criminal used to stand. Another such block is on the eastern side, and there the accuser stood.

The Pnyx is a lower hill, where public meetings were held at daybreak to avoid the heat. There were only a few wooden benches there. The people stood or sat on the bare rocks.

The Museum was where the poet Musæus was buried.

The first houses were built on the Acropolis. Afterwards men set up their dwellings on the plain below. But the Acropolis was always the citadel or fortress, the strongest part of the city.

Pisistratus was the first to think of making the Acropolis beautiful. He erected three temples and other public buildings. Xerxes, the king of the Persians, when he invaded the land, found this height surrounded by a palisade of logs, which he burned with everything else on the hill. After that no dwellings, but many splendid temples and monuments, were built there. More and more were added through fifty years in the days of Themistocles, Cimon, and Pericles. Athens had then become the most magnificent city in Greece.

On the Acropolis stood three temples devoted to Athene. One held an image of the goddess made of olive wood, which was said to have fallen from heaven, and was the most sacred thing in Athens. This was called Athene Polias, and every four years a grand procession marched up the hill to put upon the statue an elegant new robe which the women had embroidered.

The plain on which the lower part of the city stood is rocky and barren. However, a line of olive trees reached from the river Cephissus to the sea. The air is very clear and pure, so that the people lived much out of doors. At sunset the hills around glow with different colors, violet, rose, and molten gold.

Three miles from Athens was the harbor called the Piræus. It had three openings, made narrow by walls built out into the water so that not more than two large boats could pass at once. In time of war these openings were closed by chains stretched across them. Long walls, fourteen or fifteen feet thick, were built all the way from the city down to the water's edge, and the citizens took great pride in their strength.

The Piræus was really the name of three places,— first the peninsula or point of land itself, second the harbor and third the town which grew up around the harbor. Themistocles built the walls around the port, and Pericles continued them all the way up to the city.

Lysander, the Spartan conqueror, pulled them

down, but they were rebuilt. Many years afterwards, when the Romans came and conquered, they tore down the walls and forts and left Athens without protection.

Even then, when she had no power in the war, she was still honored as the most learned city in the world. For hundreds of years it was the fashion for young men to go there for education in philosophy, literature, and art. The Romans admired the splendid city and did much to add to its beauty.

CHAPTER XXXIV

THE BOY AND THE FOX

ALTHOUGH Sparta was one of the smallest of the Greek states, it became one of the most famous. This was because one of its great men, Lycurgus, gave it laws of unusual excellence. That he might do this, he traveled in many countries and noticed everything that was best in their government.

When he went home again he drew up the constitution, a body of laws obedience to which made the Spartans brave, strong, patient, and victorious.

He found that a few citizens owned all the land, while many had no estate. By his rules the land was equally divided so that every family had a small farm. Each farm would yield, in a year, about seventy bushels of grain for a man and twelve bushels for his wife, besides olives for oil and grapes for wine. In that way nobody could become very rich, and nobody had any excuse for being a beggar.

Lycurgus then tried to divide among the people all the money, jewelry, handsome dresses, and rich furniture that were in the country. But those who owned such things would not give them up. So he tried another way to keep everybody poor. He would not allow any gold or silver coins to be used. The only money the Spartans had was iron, and that was very cheap, so that a man wishing to carry a hundred dollars with him must own or hire a cart and a yoke of oxen. That put a stop to nearly all stealing, for robbers could not easily escape with their ill-gotten gains.

Yet on the other hand the Spartan children were taught to steal anything they could carry. Lycurgus said the habit would be useful in time of war. When they were in an enemy's country the Spartan soldiers could in that way get food and money. To them the only disgrace in stealing was in being found out.

Lycurgus did not wish his people to be friendly with strangers. Foreigners were not invited to come and do business in Sparta or to live there. Spartans were not to be merchants, or traders, or travelers. They were to stay at home and be good citizens and soldiers. The only time for travel was when they went out to fight their enemies.

Every child, when only a few days old, was carried before a company of wise old men. They looked at it carefully. If it was deformed, or if it seemed sickly, it was not allowed to live. Every Spartan was expected to be strong and well. Only plain and wholesome food was eaten. Nothing rich or dainty was allowed.

Little boys stayed at home with their mothers until they were seven years old. Then the state took charge of them and trained them in gymnastics and in the art of war. Their daily exercise was jumping, running, wrestling, playing at quoits and with lances. They were treated roughly and cruelly, but they were taught not to complain. They were not thought to be men until they were thirty years old; from that time until they were sixty years old they were obliged to serve the state. Only the women, the children under seven and the men over sixty ate at home. All others, even though married, had to eat at the public tables. They sat down in companies of fifteen persons, and the same kind of food was served to all. The favorite dish was a "black broth," which only Spartans liked.

In their festivals the Spartans had three choirs, one of old men, one of young men, and one of boys. The old men sang,

"Once in battle bold we shone."

The young men chanted,

"Try us; our vigor is not gone."

Then the boys ended with the chorus,

"The palm remains for us alone."

The Spartans had slaves called Helots, who did all the rough and coarse work. They were permitted to get drunk, and when they were in that condition Spartan fathers called their sons and said, "See! Thus slaves may drink and thus they may behave, but such a condition and such action are not for freemen or the sons of freemen."

Spartan women were taught to be almost as fierce and warlike as the men. When the young men were going to war, each mother gave her son a shield and said, "Come back with this or on it." If he was defeated and lost his shield, above all if he threw it away and ran from the field, he was forever disgraced. Those who were killed in battle were laid, each upon his shield, by his comrades, and carried home in honor as heroes.

It is very strange that when they marched to fight they did not blow trumpets. They charged to the soft, sweet music of flutes. It was their boast that they did not need loud noise to make them brave.

Their character is shown in the story of the boy and the fox. The little fellow on his way to school saw some fox cubs playing together. They belonged to a man who was fond of pets. The boy picked one up and hiding it under his coat went on to school. The fox, restless and angry, began to gnaw the boy's flesh just above the heart. The child studied his lessons without a word or cry, though he grew pale and weak. Suddenly he sank down upon the ground, and when the teacher went to him and opened his coat, the fox jumped out and ran away. But the boy was dead. He could steal and suffer and die rather than be found out. That was the Spartan idea of manliness.

CHAPTER XXXV

THE OLYMPIC GAMES

THE Greeks were very fond of athletic games. The greatest of these were held once every four years at a place called Olympia.

How early these games began to be celebrated nobody knows. They had fallen out of use for some time when Iphitus, a friend of Lycurgus and king of Elis, gave them a new start. From that time on for hundreds of years they were very popular.

They began on the day of the first full moon after the 21st of June. Four days were given to the games; on the fifth day there were processions, sacrifices, and banquets in honor of those who had won the prizes.

All wars were stopped for the whole month in which the games took place. It was to be a time of peace and pleasure for everybody.

No Barbarian, or slave, or man who had broken the laws, could take part. The Greeks called all foreigners, Barbarians. Women were not allowed even to see the games. If any woman did so, she was thrown from the top of a high rock. Women, however, could send chariots to the races, and sometimes won a prize.

There were twenty-four different events, divided among the four days. Eighteen were for men, six for boys.

First was a foot race, second a double foot race twice around the ring, third a still longer race. The fourth event was wrestling, the fifth was the pentathlon, which included a long jump, a foot race, throwing the quoit, throwing the spear, and wrestling. Sixth came boxing, seventh a chariot race for four horses, eighth the pancratium, which was boxing and wrestling, ninth a horse race, tenth and eleventh a foot race and wrestling for boys. The twelfth was the pentathlon for boys. Then there were chariot races with mules, with two horses, with four colts, with two colts, a foot race of heavy-armed soldiers, and pancratium, or boxing and wrestling, for boys.

Sometimes there were only two judges, sometimes eight, or ten, or even twelve. It was their duty to see that all the laws of the games were kept and to give the prizes. They wore purple robes and had reserved seats in the best place. They took solemn oath to be just and fair.

In foot races, running, leaping, boxing, and wrestling, the poorest citizens could take part as freely as the richest. But every one who entered had spent ten months in careful training, and faithfully promised to do everything fairly and to use no tricks or deceptions.

Owners of chariots were not obliged to drive,

but could hire men for that purpose. Alcibiades once sent seven chariots and won three prizes.

The prizes were only wreaths of wild olive, cut from a sacred tree that grew near by. Palm branches were also placed in the hands of the victors.

When a man or a boy won a prize, his name, the name of his father and of his country were called out by heralds. He was invited to the great banquet given by the people of Elis to the winners. He was considered to have honored his city, and when he went home a procession met him, and songs in praise of him were sung.

A statue of him was carved from stone and set up in the highest place at Olympia. This was not a city, but a spot full of temples and altars to the gods and statues of the victors in the games.

People journeyed to these exhibitions from all parts of Greece and from many foreign lands. Deputies were sent from different cities, each of whom tried to dress more splendidly and to make a finer display than his neighbor.

A great deal of business was done in buying and selling. All kinds of goods could be bought there, and it was like a huge fair.

Painters showed their pictures, and poets and historians read their works before the crowd. This helped to educate the people, who had not many books, and who would rather listen than read for themselves.

Those were times of great enjoyment, and the

Greeks took much pleasure in them. The year of the games and the three following years were called an Olympiad, and time was measured by them. Events were said to have happened in the fifth, or twentieth, or fiftieth, or any other Olympiad.

Other games like these were held in different parts of Greece at various times, but none of them were so splendid or so interesting as the Olympic games.

CHAPTER XXXVI

TWO GREAT LAWGIVERS

L IFE in Greece grew busy and earnest. Changes of every kind took place. The people were not satisfied to be governed by a few men; they themselves wished to share in the government. There were no written laws, but everything was done according to old custom.

About six hundred years before Christ, Draco, the greatest man of the nobility, was chosen to write down a system of laws by which all people were to be ruled. In those laws nearly every crime was punished with death. There was no difference between the punishment of a man who stole a loaf of bread and that of a murderer. It was a common saying that Draco wrote his laws, not in ink, but in blood. The people were not satisfied with these laws, and a greater and wiser lawgiver was found.

This was Solon, who belonged to a rich family in Athens. He received all the education of the time at the gymnasium and in the schools. His one great desire was to learn; and after leaving school he traveled as a merchant on his own ship, that he might see the world and find out all he could about its people. He loved his country, and all his studies were intended to help him give to his native land more freedom and greater power.

Some years before Solon's time the island of Salamis had rebelled against Athens and put itself under the protection of Megara. Several times the Athenians had sent ships and men to conquer the island, but they had always been defeated. The people were so ashamed of this that they passed a law that any man who proposed an expedition against Salamis should be put to death.

Solon was angry. He was a poet, and he wrote a poem of a hundred lines upon the loss of the island. To escape death he pretended to be crazy and rushed into the market place with wild looks and disordered garments. A crowd gathered around him, and he began to recite his poem. His voice, his looks, his manner, and his words aroused the Athenians to fury. These were the closing lines of the poem:—

"Up! and to Salamis on! Let us fight for the beautiful island,
Angrily down to the dust casting the yoke of our shame."

When he had finished the men of Athens rushed from the market place, crowded on board the ships, sailed to Salamis, and conquered it again for Athens.

Solon was then the popular hero and favorite. His word was law. To bring the people into closer friendship he ordered a change in worship. Until then Apollo had been the god of the nobility, and they alone had the right to worship him. Solon consecrated to him the city and the state. Every house was made sacred to that god, and a statue of him was set up in every street. New prayers and hymns were written to be used in the religious services. Fires were lighted upon the altars, and the citizens, putting laurel wreaths upon their heads, marched in procession to the temples. They said to one another, "We are all brothers; let us live like brothers in friendship and love."

Solon might now have made himself the only ruler of Attica and Athens, but that was not his wish. He drew up a system of laws which he thought would help the state to be happy, peaceful, and successful.

Times had been hard in Athens. Many people had fallen into debt, and some had become so poor that they had been sold as slaves. Solon made a law that no citizen should own another, and that no one should be sold into slavery because he was poor. Thus thousands were set free, and thousands more were saved from misery.

He lowered the rate of interest and altered the value of the currency, so that if a man owed a hundred dollars he could pay his debt with seventy-three dollars. The state was to forgive all who owed it money and to free them from the burden of such debts.

He set aside all the laws of Draco, except those which punished murder. He divided the citizens into four classes, according to the land they owned. Only the first class, who were richest in land, could hold high office in the state or in the army. The second and third classes might have some of the lower offices, and their taxes were made very light. In war, men of the second class must serve as cavalry, of the third class as heavy-armed foot soldiers. Men of the fourth class could not hold office, but they paid no taxes. They had a right to vote at the public meetings where officers were elected and new laws were passed. In war they were sailors, or light-armed foot soldiers. In that way every freeman helped to govern and to defend the state.

Solon also changed the laws of the family. No man had a right to sell his child, or to drive him away from home while under age. If the father would not educate the child, he was not allowed to receive any help from him when his son had grown to be a man.

He did not permit any Athenian to make or sell ointment, for he said that such a business was unmanly. Very expensive dress was forbidden, and only a certain sum of money could be spent for a wedding or a funeral, or for a monument over the dead. Wild crying for those who died came into fashion, but Solon said it was useless and foolish and could no longer be allowed.

All these laws were put into writing and placed on pillars upon the citadel, or highest point of the city, that everybody might read them. These pillars were of wood, as tall as a man, and shaped like a pyramid.

Then Solon ordered a general peace. Those who had been banished from the city were invited to return; no man was to be called a rebel or a traitor; the past was to be forgotten; kindness and helpfulness were to be the rule of life.

When his year of office was over, Solon went away for ten years and traveled into Egypt and Asia. Kings and princes were glad to see him and talk with him, for all said that he was the greatest lawmaker in the world.

CHAPTER XXXVII

THE RING OF POLYCRATES

H ERODOTUS, the famous historian, tells this story:—

Polycrates was ruler of the island of Samos. He had raised an insurrection against the Persians and taken the government into his own hands. To increase his power, he sent gifts to Amasis, king of Egypt, and made with him a treaty of friendship.

He sent into other countries for the best workmen, to whom he paid high wages, and set them to work at building splendid temples. His palace was richly furnished with splendid hangings, and he had many cups and dishes of silver and gold. These he lent to any of his citizens who wished to hold a wedding or to give a great feast.

He was very fond of animals and brought into Samos the finest kinds of sheep, goats, and pigs.

The fabled Argo was said to have seats for fifty rowers, and tradition called her the largest vessel in the world. Polycrates had a fleet of one hundred fifty-oared galleys, with which he sailed from island to island, robbing friends and foes.

Good fortune followed him everywhere. It seemed as if nobody could defeat him in battle or get the better of him in trade.

The king of Egypt, knowing this, began to be afraid that his friend would come to a dreadful end. He sent a letter to Polycrates, telling him that such continual good fortune was a token that the gods were keeping him for some terrible fate and advising him to throw away his most valuable treasure.

"In that way," said Amasis, "thou mayest escape punishment from the beings who rule the world, and who do not like to see any man too prosperous."

Polycrates decided that his dearest treasure was a signet-ring of emerald set in gold. This he determined to throw away and therefore ordered one of his fifty-oared galleys to be made ready for sea. Going on board he sailed a long way from the island, and, with great sorrow, threw the ring into the deep waters.

A few days afterwards, as he sat in his palace, a fisherman came to the gate and asked to see the king. Polycrates having permitted him to enter, beheld in his hands a large and beautiful fish.

"O king!" said the fisherman, "I am a poor man who lives by his trade, yet, when I saw this prize in my nets I said that it should not be sold, but that I would give it to the great king in whose waters it was taken."

Polycrates was pleased and answered, "Thou hast

THE KING AND THE FISHERMAN

done well, my friend. Come to supper with me and help me to eat thy gift."

The servants took the fish and began to make it ready for the table. When they opened it they saw, shining before them, the ring their master had thrown away!

The king was glad to have his ring again, and he wrote a letter to Amasis, telling him of this new piece of good fortune.

The king of Egypt sent an answer saying that they could no longer be friends, because he did not dare to keep a treaty of friendship with a man who was always fortunate.

A Persian named Orœtes was governor of Sardis. He had never seen Polycrates, but hearing much of him he determined to match himself against that fortunate king, and, if possible, to destroy him.

He was wise enough to see that this could only be done by treachery. He wrote a letter in which he pretended to be afraid of losing his power and his life, and begged Polycrates to come to his rescue. In return he offered to share his great treasures with his deliverer, and promised to show his money and jewels to any one whom the king would send for the purpose of ascertaining that they were genuine.

Polycrates was glad of these offers and sent his secretary to make sure that it was all true. Orœtes had nearly filled eight chests with stones, over which he had laid gold in money and in bars. These he showed to the secretary, who, only seeing what was before his eyes, went home and told the king that he had seen great treasures, and that the Persian was really very rich.

Polycrates declared that he himself would go and bring away the governor and his money. Many friends begged him not to be so foolish. His daughter had a dream, in which she saw her father high in the air, "washed by Zeus and anointed by the sun." She tried to keep him at home, for she believed that this dream meant some dreadful danger for her father. But he did not listen to her prayers or care for her tears. He sailed away with a company of friends, but without his army, thinking that his good fortune would not forsake him.

He had fallen into a trap. The Persian governor killed him, and then nailed his dead body to a cross. As he hung high in the air Zeus might be said to wash him with rain, and the sun to anoint him by pouring over him powerful rays. The poor girl's dream was fulfilled, and the fortunate Polycrates came to a miserable end.

CHAPTER XXXVIII

"I WILL BE GREATEST"

A YOUNG man said, "I will rule Athens and be the greatest man within her walls." This youth was named Pisistratus.

His mother was first cousin to Solon's mother. He and Solon were friends, and when the lawgiver led the attack on Salamis, this young man fought by his side. His father left him plenty of money, a fine house, large and beautiful gardens. He had a handsome face, a noble form, a rich voice, and a powerful mind. Knowing that he had these gifts, he was determined to be the ruler and leader of his native city.

There were three parties in Athens, each trying to gain and hold the governing power. The rich landowners called themselves "the Plain." "The Coast" party were men who were rich, but not noble. The other party, who called themselves "the Highlands," were in favor of freedom and equality. To this party most of the poor belonged. Pisistratus joined them, for he thought they had most votes. To please the people he opened his gardens to everybody.

He said, "Why should I keep for myself all these shady walks, these marble statues, these cool and sparkling fountains? If they are mine, that only gives me the right to say that the people of Athens shall enjoy them. The gates shall not be closed. The lanes, the paths, the seats, are free to the public."

When he walked out he had with him two or three young men, whom he called his purse-bearers. They gave money to every poor man they met.

He was a brave soldier and a good speaker, and the people liked him for this and for his generosity. He became the leading citizen of Athens. Many men who were opposed to him were banished.

One day he went into the market-place, wounded and bleeding. He declared that his enemies had attacked him while riding in the country. Solon said that the wounds were very slight, and that Pisistratus had cut and stabbed himself.

But the people cried out, "Let the friend of the people have a bodyguard. Let him have fifty men with clubs to go with him everywhere."

This was ordered, but Pisistratus raised a much larger force, took the citadel, and was master of Athens.

A number of citizens left the city. Solon took his helmet, spear, and sword, and laid them down in the street before the door of his house. "I can do no more," he said to the people. "You would not listen to me. There are my arms, no longer of any use."

Pisistratus made no change in the laws and governed well, but his enemies finally drove him out, and he was gone six years. Then one of the leaders went to him and said, "Marry my daughter, and I will take you back to Athens and to power." He agreed, and this was their plan. They found a very tall and beautiful country girl, a garland seller, whom they dressed in armor like Athene. She entered a chariot with Pisistratus and drove toward Athens. Heralds went before, shouting, "Ye men of Athens, the great goddess Athene is coming, and with her is your beloved leader and true friend." The people believed this, and Pisistratus became again the ruler.

He did not treat his wife well, and her father, with others, drove him out again.

For ten years he tried to get back. The Greek cities gave him money, Thebes giving most of all. At last he landed with an army at Marathon. Friends hurried to him; his enemies marched out to meet him. The two camps were near together. The Athenians ate their dinner; then some of the soldiers went to sleep, while others played ball. Pisistratus led his troops against them and they ran like frightened sheep.

He did not follow, but sent his sons on horseback to say, "Have no fear, go quietly home, and you shall not be disturbed." They obeyed, and Pisistratus entered Athens, never to leave it while he lived.

His enemies, of course, were driven away. But he obeyed the laws, and made everybody else obey. He sent poor people out of the city to work on farms, and gave oxen and seed to those who had none. Other poor men he employed in erecting temples and public buildings.

He laid out a public garden called the Lyceum, built a splendid fountain over the "Nine Springs," founded a free public library, and gave pensions to men hurt in the wars.

He ordered the religious festivals to be well observed, brought Thespis and his actors from the country into the city, and gathered into one book the songs and poems of Homer. Peace, beauty, order, and gladness filled the city during the rest of his long life. He had kept his word that he would be the greatest man in Athens. When he died his son Hippias took his place.

CHAPTER XXXIX

THE POETS

THE finest poems which have come to us from the Greeks are the *Iliad* and the *Odyssey*. Formerly these were supposed to have been written by Homer. Old stories tell us that this poet was born in the island of Chios (now called Scio), a thousand years before the birth of Christ; that he was blind, and that he sang his songs and begged his way through seven cities, each of which, after he was dead, claimed to be the place of his birth.

Scholars who have studied the matter say that this account cannot be true. They declare that these wonderful poems are not all the work of one man, but were written by many different persons and at different times. In their original form they were sung by wandering minstrels at the great festivals. Those who sang them added to them from time to time. At first they were not written, because writing was then unknown in Greece, but were repeated from memory by the singers. In that way they had been known and sung for more than five hundred years.

Then Pisistratus had them written down, as we

now have them, in two volumes, which he placed in the public library established by him at Athens.

The first of these volumes, called the *Iliad*, tells about some things that happened in the last year of the Trojan war. The second volume, the *Odyssey*, describes the wanderings of Ulysses, king of Ithaca, after the war and before he reached his home.

However these poems came into being, there is no question about their beauty and power. Many learned men think there is nothing equal to them in the world. An English writer has said, "If you read Homer, you will not want to read anything else, nor do you need any other books."

Though most people know what is believed to be the truth about Homer, he is always spoken of as if he were a real person and actually composed the poems which bear his name.

Another poet who wrote about a hundred years later than Homer was Hesiod. One of his works was about farming and sailing and the common things of life; the other was the family history of the gods, telling of their births, marriages, and adventures.

Three great tragic poets were Æschylus, Sophocles, and Euripides.

The greatest comic poet was Aristophanes, who made fun of real people.

Theocritus of Sicily wrote beautiful poems about country life.

Anacreon wrote about love and wine. He is said to have been choked by a grape seed.

There were many lyric poets, who wrote songs to be sung at the games and festivals. Simonides, who lived at the time of the Persian war, was one of these. When the victors came home he wrote songs in their praise, which made them prouder than ever that they had served their country so well. For those who had died in battle he wrote hymns, which made their friends glad that they had known and loved such heroes. His songs of sorrow brought tears to many eyes. He won fifty prizes for his poetry at different times. The last he gained was at Athens, when he was nearly eighty years old. After that he went to Syracuse, and lived there ten years longer, being almost ninety when he died.

Pindar was another famous writer of songs. He was sent to Athens to study. When he was twenty years old he went to Thebes and began to write. He found two women there who also wrote beautiful songs, and who taught him much about poetry. One of these was named Corinna.

The different states of Greece paid him to write songs to be sung in chorus after a great victory, or at some other time of rejoicing. After the Persian wars he composed a poem in praise of Athens, which pleased the citizens so well that they gave him a valuable present, and after his death set up a statue in his honor.

He liked to be among kings and great people, but his nature was sincere, manly, and generous.

He wrote poems for victors, hymns to the gods,

solemn dirges for the dead, and merry songs to be sung at feasts.

He had many friends everywhere. Sometimes he was called the Theban eagle. When Alexander the Great captured Thebes he pulled down every house except the one in which Pindar had lived many years before. In that way he showed respect to the poet whose writings he knew and liked.

Alcæus, a citizen of the island of Lesbos, was also a lyric poet. He wrote short poems about love and music; others in honor of events or of persons.

Terpander, who also lived at Lesbos, invented a better harp for the use of minstrels who sang the Homeric hymns, which were written by other poets who lived after the days of Homer.

Sappho, of Lesbos, wrote poems, and gave lessons in poetry and music to the women of Asia Minor. Plato called her the tenth muse; and Solon, having heard her recite one of her poems, prayed that he might not die until he had committed it to memory. She is said to have been in love with Phaon, who did not care for her. To cure herself of hopeless love, she leaped from the top of a rock into the sea and so died.

Archilochus was born in the island of Paros. He came from a poor family; it is even said that his mother was a slave. But his mind was full of beautiful thoughts, and he wrote songs about war and freedom,—songs which helped other men to be brave and noble.

CHAPTER XL

THE THREE ORDERS OF ARCHITECTURE

EARLY men, who lived long before the Greeks, made their homes in caves. These men were hunters and perhaps fishermen. When they learned to cultivate the soil, and so had become farmers, they found out how to make dwellings of branches of trees woven together, or of dried sods piled up to form a rude hut.

Men who lived by the milk and flesh of flocks of sheep and goats needed light dwellings which they could easily carry about. They learned to sew together the skins of animals and thus to make tents, which were moved from place to place as the flocks moved.

In rocky countries where loose stones were plenty the inhabitants learned to build huts by piling stones together, so making a kind of artificial cave. People who lived on wide plains where there were no rocks, learned to make bricks of clay. At first these bricks were dried in the sun, as they still are in some countries. Later the art of baking them in a kiln was discovered.

Men who lived in forests built their huts first of wattled or interwoven branches, then of logs. The Greeks were always stone builders. They began by using large, rough blocks rudely fitted together. Then they chiseled the blocks into irregular forms. At last they cut the stones into six-sided blocks and laid them up in regular courses.

We can see that the love of order and beauty was growing in the minds of the Greeks. They did not try to imitate the buildings they had seen in other countries, but developed styles of their own.

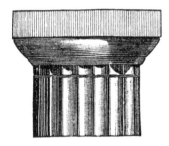

DORIC CAPITAL

The first style we should naturally expect to be plain and simple. This was called the Doric order. Perhaps it arose from imitating the rude log temples of an older time in an earlier settled country when the columns, or pillars, of temples were made of logs. It was said, however, that these Doric pillars were modeled after a man's figure, being six times as high as they were thick, just as a man is about six times as tall as his foot is long.

IONIC CAPITAL

The Ionians, another tribe of the Greeks, were building a temple to Artemis, and wished to find some new and beautiful way. So they made a column like a woman; that is, more slender than a man. At the base they put twisted cords like a woman's sandals; and the top, or capital, they curled over, like a woman's hair on each side of her face. This style was called the Ionic order.

At Corinth a young girl died. A basket of flowers was placed on her grave, and upon it a tile was laid to keep it from being blown over. This pressed the flowers down and made them curl over the sides of the basket.

CORINTHIAN CAPITAL

An architect, who was walking in the cemetery, saw this and thought it would make a beautiful capital, or top, for a pillar. He had the design carved in stone and used it in the next temple he built. This style is called the Corinthian order.

Many modern buildings show one or other of these three orders. The Corinthian is the favorite, because it is considered most graceful and beautiful.

The temple of the Parthenon at Athens was of the Doric order, and was one of the finest buildings in the world. When it was built the Corinthian order was unknown.

The Greeks used very fine white marble for their

statues and buildings. Often they ornamented them with color and with gold. This added to their beauty, and beauty was what the Grecians dearly loved.

CHAPTER XLI

WITH CHISEL AND PENCIL

NEARLY all nations in old times worshiped idols, that is, images of their gods. They did not exactly believe that such images were the gods themselves; yet they thought that somehow the god was nearer when they could see and perhaps touch his image. At first, when the Greeks were little more than savages, they took stone or a log of wood and set it up under a tree or in a little house, and said, "This is sacred to the god Hermes," or to the goddess Athene, or to some other deity. "We will pray before it, and the god will listen, and give us what we ask." They would bring flowers or fruits or shells from the seaside, or any strange or pretty things, and lay them down before the stone or log as a present to their god.

After a long time men began to shape the log or the stone. They carved the likeness of a head at the upper end, and that made the idol look a little more like something alive. Then they could put a dress on its shoulders, and a crown on its head, or a necklace around its neck. This did not satisfy their love for the beautiful. They kept on trying to make images more pleasing to themselves and to their gods. They gave up wood and used the finest white marble. This they carved with great patience, giving form not only to the head and neck and shoulders, but to the body and to every limb. "Practice makes perfect," you know, and every year they learned to do this work better.

At the same time they were learning to erect grand buildings of the white marble. These were not for their own use but were intended to be temples; that is, places where their gods should be worshiped. Each temple had a room in which the statue of its god was placed, and the building was called after his name. It was the temple of Zeus, or of Apollo, or of Poseidon; perhaps of Hera, or of Aphrodite. There altars were set up, and upon them priests offered the gifts brought by the people.

When the Greeks found they could do so well their work of building and carving, they took more interest and tried harder. They learned that instead of chiseling the figure at once out of rock, they could do better by modeling it in soft clay and copying it in marble. In that way they made not only single figures but groups; these they placed in different parts of the temples, not to be worshiped but to be admired. They also learned to cast figures in bronze and gold.

After a while when people grew richer and built fine houses to live in, they had likenesses of themselves and of their wives and children, as well as of the gods, carved and set up in their homes. They adorned their public places with images of famous soldiers and of winners in the great games. No other country in the world had so many beautiful statues as Greece.

Those who make such statues are called "sculptors." The greatest of these was Phidias, who lived at Athens nearly two thousand four hundred years ago. He will always be famous for his great statue of Zeus, which he made of gold and ivory and which stood in the temple at Olympia. It was one of the seven wonders of the world. At Athens he made a splendid figure of Athene. Her face and hands and feet were of ivory; her dress was of solid gold.

Phidias was also a painter; and there were many others. Their work was generally done upon the inside walls of houses and temples. They were fond of battle scenes which told stories of great wars; but they also made fine pictures of country life and sports. The earliest paintings were probably upon jars or vases.

Two of the famous painters were Parrhasius and Zeuxis. There were often disputes as to which was the better artist, and to settle that point it was agreed to have a public exhibition of their work. Zeuxis sent a picture of juicy grapes, and while the people were looking at it some birds flew down and pecked at the painted fruit. Everybody shouted with surprise and pleasure. Then Zeuxis said,—

"Come, Parrhasius, draw aside the curtain that hangs in front of your picture and let us see what you have painted."

Parrhasius smiled but did not stir. Zeuxis became impatient.

THE BIRDS DECEIVED

"You trifle with us. Why do you not draw the curtain?" he said.

"Look closer," replied the other artist.

The people crowded up; Zeuxis with them. They saw that there was no curtain except the picture itself.

"Parrhasius has won," everybody shouted. "Parrhasius has won!"

"It is true!" said Zeuxis. "He has fairly won. My art could deceive the birds, but he has done more for he has deceived an artist!"

Hundreds of years afterwards, in the days of Alexander the Great, there was a famous artist, by many considered the greatest, named Apelles. He painted a likeness of Alexander about to throw a thunderbolt. For this picture he was paid a large sum of money, and Alexander declared that no one else should ever paint his portrait.

Apelles was always willing to learn. Before he finished a picture he would place it in front of his house and hide near by, that he might hear the remarks of those who passed along the street. One day a cobbler found fault with the shoes of a figure. Apelles changed them as the shoemaker had suggested. This encouraged the cobbler, who on another day declared that the legs of the man were badly painted. Apelles knew that was not true. He came from behind the picture, and said, "Stick to your last, cobbler, stick to your last." By that he meant that men should only find fault with what they clearly understand to be wrong.

187

CHAPTER XLII

THE BATTLE OF MARATHON

DARIUS king of Persia, ruled the largest empire in the world at that time. He had conquered much of Greece but some cities still kept their independence. He sent among them heralds, who cried out, "Your mighty master, Darius, is king of Persia and of the world. Send him earth and water, that he may know that you yield to his goodness and submit to his power."

Some of the smaller states obeyed, but Athens and Sparta refused. They threw one herald into a deep pit and said, "Take all the earth you want." Another they cast into a river and said, "There is plenty of water; help yourself!"

Darius was very angry. He raised an army of 120,000 men, put them on board of 600 ships, and sent them to the shores of Greece. They landed and marched on to Marathon, only twenty miles from Athens.

The Athenians sent to the Platæans and the Spartans for help. Platæa sent a thousand men,—all the soldiers the city had.

But the Spartans said, "It will not be full moon for several days yet. We cannot march until the moon is full. Wait until then, and we will help you."

The Athenians could not wait. They marched out of their city and encamped on the hills around the plain of Marathon. They had only ten thousand men, and there were ten generals. Five of these wished to wait until the Spartans could come to help them; but one, named Miltiades, insisted that they should go immediately into battle. It had been agreed that each general should command for one day and then give place to another; but they changed their plan. Some one said, "Let Miltiades alone be the leader. He asks us to fight now and we will do so. Make him our commander and we will follow him every day and everywhere."

The whole army shouted, "Miltiades! Let only Miltiades lead us!"

He waited until his day of command arrived and then gave the order to march.

The Persians were stretched across the plain. Their best and bravest troops were in the center. Behind them was the beach with their ships lying close to shore. At each end of the plain were deep marshes.

Miltiades put his weakest soldiers in the center while the strongest and bravest were at the sides. The armies were a mile apart. The Greeks charged fiercely upon the enemy, who were more than ten times as many. The brave fighters in the Persian center soon drove back the Greeks, but the men at the wings, or sides, of the foreign army were thrown into confusion by the fierce

Greek warriors and ran toward their boats. Many of them fell into the marshes and were drowned.

Miltiades called together his scattered men and marched swiftly against the Persian center. Those soldiers thought that they had already won the fight and were surprised when the Greeks came running upon them. They too fled to their ships, but many were killed and many were lost in the marshes. More than six thousand never reached the vessels, and seven of the ships were destroyed by the Greeks. The Athenians lost only one hundred and ninety-two men. It was a sudden and complete victory.

It is said that the people at Athens first heard the news from a wounded soldier. They were gathered in the market place when this man, bloody and dusty, burst in among them. He had run all the way, twenty miles, to tell the good tidings.

"What news, soldier?" the people cried. "How goes the day? Are we safe, or are the Persians marching now upon our city?"

The soldier drew himself up to his full height and shook his hand in the air. "Victory!" he cried. "Rejoice, Athenians, our city is saved!" Then he fell dead into the extended arms of his fellow-citizens.

The people believed that the gods had helped them. They said that before the battle began many heard the voice of the great Pan among the mountains, cheering the soldiers forward and promising to them the victory.

TIDINGS FROM MARATHON

Others declared that in the thickest of the fight they had seen Theseus in full armor using his sword against the Persians. No sound followed the blow, but whoever was struck went down and rose no more. Persian spears and arrows fell harmless upon his tall helmet and shining breastplate.

Some said they saw the mighty Heracles with his club driving the Persians into the sea as a shepherd drives his flock into the fold.

The battle of Marathon has always been considered one of the greatest ever fought in the land of Greece. Miltiades was given the highest honors. His statue was set up in a public place; everybody praised him; he was the most popular man in Athens.

Afterwards, with a fleet of seventy vessels, he attacked a town on the island of Paros. He was defeated and wounded. It was proved that he had used the soldiers and ships of Athens against his own private enemy. For this he was fined fifty talents, or sixty thousand dollars, instead of being put to death. He could not pay the money, but was kept in prison and soon died there of his wound. His son Cimon raised the money for the fine and gave his father's body honorable burial.

CHAPTER XLIII

THE GREATEST ARMY

D ARIUS did not forgive or forget his great defeat at Marathon. He spent three years in gathering an army larger than the first, but before he could lead it against Greece he died. His son Xerxes became king, and during four more years was busy in collecting soldiers and building ships. When all was ready he set out upon the march, thinking that he would punish the Greeks for the disgrace and shame which they had made his father suffer.

At Abydos he held a great review of his army. He had ordered a throne of white marble to be built on a hill which was near the city and which overlooked both land and sea. There he sat and saw his vessels covering the narrow sea called the Hellespont, and his soldiers filling the shore and the plains about Abydos. At first he was glad and proud, but after a while he burst into tears.

When his uncle heard of this he went to him, and said, "O king and lord! why are your feelings changed? Not long ago you were smiling and happy because your greatness lay before you. Nothing is altered, and yet your eyes are dim and your face is wet with tears. Why this sudden change?"

The king replied, "When I saw this great company of men a sudden pity came upon me to think that human life is so short, and that of all these soldiers not one will be alive in a hundred years."

But that thought did not prevent him from leading these men to war, in which many thousands of them died in a few weeks.

The Hellespont is three miles wide at Abydos. Xerxes had a bridge of boats built that his armies might cross. A storm arose, broke up the bridge, and scattered the boats. The king was furious.

"Take whips," he cried out, "take whips, and lash those waves that dare to rise against me! Throw chains into those waters and bind them to my will! I am their master and they shall obey me."

When the storm was over two new bridges of boats were built and the army marched safely across into Thrace. It was the largest company of soldiers the world had ever seen. It had been gathered from every part of the Persian empire, which included forty-six different nations of Asia and Africa. Some were barbarians and dressed in skins; others were in shining brass armor; others wore light, thin clothing suited to a hot climate. Some had their bodies painted, half red and half white. One tribe had arrows tipped with stone instead of iron.

In the wide plain of Doriscus the Persian king

commanded that his army should be counted. It was done in this way: ten thousand men were numbered and ordered to stand together as closely as possible. A line was drawn around the spot on which they stood, and the soldiers were marched away. Then a wall was built to enclose the space marked by the line. That space was filled one hundred and seventy times before the whole army had been included; making a total of 1,700,000 men. There were also 80,000 horses, a number of war chariots and many camels, with about 20,000 men as drivers and caretakers.

There was a fleet of 1,207 triremes and 3,000 smaller vessels. The triremes were galleys with three rows of oars on each side. Each of these vessels had 200 rowers and 30 fighting-men on board. The lesser vessels had each eight men.

As this great army marched from Doriscus toward Thermopylæ it was joined by soldiers from Thrace, Macedonia, and other nations. Other war galleys were also added to the fleet; so that by land and sea the Persians brought against the Greeks many more than two millions of fighting-men. There were also slaves, crews of the provision vessels, and other men of various kinds, so that Herodotus says the total number was 5,283,220.

Many writers think this cannot possibly be true, but it is certain that it was the largest army ever brought together in the history of the world.

As they marched Xerxes sent messages to the principal cities along their road, requiring each to furnish a day's food for the army. This cost so much that several cities were nearly ruined. The island of Thasos, which owned property on the mainland, was compelled to spend in this way what would equal nearly 500,000 dollars in our money.

While Xerxes was making preparations to conquer Greece, a congress of the Greek states was held at Corinth. Some were afraid of the Persians and others were jealous of Athens and Sparta; so that those two cities were left almost alone to meet and fight the invader. Their brave citizens resolved to resist Xerxes to the utmost of their power. At the worst they could only die, and death, they thought, was better than slavery.

An Athenian named Themistocles was the very life of the congress. His eloquent and fiery speeches aroused the courage and fixed the resolution of every one who listened to him. His hearers were determined that the Persian monarch with his army of slaves should never conquer the free men of Greece.

CHAPTER XLIV

THE BRAVE THREE HUNDRED

THERE was only one road by which Xerxes, the Persian king, could march his great army into the heart of Greece. That road lay through the Pass of Thermopylæ.

This was a narrow passage, only wide enough for a single carriage to travel. On one side was a steep mountain, on the other a broad marsh which could not be crossed by men or beasts. Then the valley opened for some distance and in this broader space were hot springs. When a traveler had passed these springs he found that the road became narrow again, and the way out was no wider than the way in. This place was called "Thermopylæ," which means, "The Gates of the Hot Springs."

The Greeks agreed that Leonidas, king of Sparta, should lead their soldiers against the mighty army of Xerxes. But only eight thousand men could be spared for this purpose; the rest were busy in keeping the festivals, which were a part of their religion.

Leonidas led his little band to the Pass of

Thermopylæ and there, behind an old wall which his men had rebuilt, he waited for the attack. Xerxes who had so many men was surprised to see so few of the Greeks gathered to fight him. He sent an officer who said, "O foolish Greeks! what can you do against the great army of our glorious king? Surrender! Give up your swords and spears."

Leonidas only said, "Come and take them."

The officer saw that some of the Spartans were at their gymnastic games while others were combing their long hair. He told king Xerxes who said, "Why, those men must be insane." But one who knew the Spartans said, "O king, they do that to show that they are not afraid of death. When they comb their hair before a battle, it means that they intend to fight until they die."

Xerxes sent another messenger who said to the Greeks, "Why should you try to stand against us? When we shoot our arrows they will darken the sun."

"That will make it cooler," answered Leonidas. "We shall fight you more comfortably in the shade."

The Persian king waited four days, then gave the order to advance. His soldiers crowded toward the narrow opening of the pass. They had short spears and shields of basketwork. The Greeks had long spears and shields of bull hide; and their muscles were like iron. The Persians fell by hundreds, by thousands, yet hardly a Greek was touched.

Xerxes had a company of picked soldiers, strong

and brave, who were called the Ten Thousand Immortals. He ordered them to march against the Greeks. They went to the pass, but many never returned. The ground was heaped with the foreign dead.

Many of the Persian soldiers then refused to go to certain death. Their officers drove them forward with whips as if they had been dogs.

All day the battle raged and the Persian loss was very great. Then Xerxes was told that a Greek traitor would lead a part of the Persian army over the mountain, so that they could get into the pass in the rear of the Greeks. Soldiers were sent with him and began their march in the night.

Leonidas heard of this. He gathered his soldiers around him and said that those who chose could go home, but that he must stay and die; and that whoever stayed with him must also die. All left him except three hundred Spartans and some Thespians and Thebans, altogether about a thousand men.

He called two of his relatives, and said, "Carry letters from me to Sparta, then your lives will be saved."

One answered, "I am not a letter carrier, but a fighter. I will stay and die."

The other replied, "My actions will tell Sparta all she cares to know."

Leonidas did not wait to be caught in a trap. He led his soldiers out against the center of the Persians and tried to fight his way through to the tent of the king.

Two brothers of Xerxes were killed, but Leonidas also fell dead upon the plain. His few remaining soldiers picked up his body and, fighting all the way, carried it with them into the pass. There they took their stand upon a little hill and fought to the last. When their spears were broken they used their swords. When those were gone they took their short daggers. Some, when they had nothing else, fought with their naked hands.

The Thebans surrendered, but all the Thespians and Spartans fell. Not one escaped. Xerxes cut off the head of Leonidas and marched on into Greece. But the people buried all the heroes in the pass, and afterwards placed over the grave of Leonidas a marble lion. His name means, "The Lion's Son;" and the world honors him and his three hundred Spartans, braver than lions, who died fighting for Greece at the "Gate of the Hot Springs."

CHAPTER XLV

THE WOODEN WALLS

THEMISTOCLES was born in Athens in the year 514 B.C. His father was an Athenian but his mother was a foreign woman. As he grew up the boy was very stubborn and hard to manage. His own way was the only way he would have.

He was very fond of composing and delivering speeches. He liked to play that he was a lawyer in the courts, and that his young companions were bad men against whom he must speak, or good men whom he must defend from false charges.

His schoolmaster used to say with a shake of the head, "Boy, you will live to be either a great blessing or a great curse."

When he became a man he went into politics, and became the leader of the party of the people, of the poor rather than of the rich. He had a rival, Aristides, whom he caused to be banished from the state as a dangerous citizen. There was no danger except to Themistocles himself. He was afraid that Aristides would be stronger than he, so he had him sent away by "ostracism."

This was a plan to get rid of citizens before they could become too powerful.

The men of a city met together in a public place, and each one might write upon a shell, or upon an earthen tablet which was called "ostracon," the name of the person whom he wished to have banished, or "ostracised." These votes were collected and counted. If there were six thousand or more the names were read over, and the man against whom the most votes had been given was sent away from the city for ten years. His property was not taken from him and at the end of that time he could come back to his home.

When the vote was taken against Aristides he met an ignorant man who said, "I cannot write. Put down upon my shell the name of Aristides."

"Has he ever injured you?" was asked. The man answered, "No. I do not even know him." "Why, then, do you vote to have him sent away?"

"Because I am tired of hearing everybody call him 'the Just.'"

Aristides wrote his own name upon the shell and gave it to this man, who did not like him because he was just and honorable. He was sent away and Themistocles had no longer reason to fear him.

At the battle of Marathon Themistocles was in great danger and fought bravely and well. But he was not pleased because he was not the chief general and so could not claim the victory as his own. He said, "I cannot sleep for thinking of the glory gained by Miltiades."

He was strongly in favor of a large navy. A great deal of money had been gained from the silver mines at Laurium. A law was about to be passed giving two dollars to every citizen, but Themistocles said it would be far better to use that money to build ships for the war then going on.

This was done and before that war was over word was brought that Xerxes, the Persian king, was getting ready to attack Greece both by land and by sea. Themistocles said, "Men of Athens, there is only one way to conquer this king; that is, by building more ships, and using them in fighting against him."

This advice was taken and in a battle at sea Xerxes was defeated. But he marched through Northern Greece burning every town he reached always coming nearer to Athens.

The people asked, "What shall we do? We are not strong enough to meet this great enemy."

Themistocles said, "Leave the city. Go on board the ships and trust in them."

They were not willing to do that, so Themistocles went to the oracle at Delphi and brought back this answer: "To you and your children only wooden walls shall remain unconquered."

The people inquired, "Where are the wooden walls?"

Themistocles replied, "They are your ships. They alone can never be conquered."

The women and children and old men left Athens

and went for safety to another city. Some, however, took refuge behind the wooden walls upon the Acropolis. The young and brave men went on board the ships to sail for Salamis.

A Spartan general had command of all the ships. He wished to take the fleet into the gulf of Corinth to be near the land army, so that they might help him or he might aid them. Themistocles declared that it would be far better to keep the vessels in the Straits of Salamis.

The Spartan general was so angry that he lifted his hand to strike Themistocles, who said, "Strike, if you will, but hear me." Then he showed how much better it would be to go to the Straits of Salamis, and all who heard him called out, "To Salamis! To Salamis!"

Xerxes ordered his ships to close both ends of the Straits that he might catch the Greeks in a trap. Aristides was then at Ægina. He went on board a small boat and in the night was rowed through the Persian fleet to the place where Themistocles had his tent on shore. He went into the tent and said, "Let us still be rivals, but let us try which can do most to save our country."

Themistocles answered, "I will try and we shall see which is the better friend to Athens."

He had ordered that every galley should have a strong iron prow, or beak, and that with these they should try to strike the enemy's vessels on the side so as to break the oars and sink the ships. His fleet numbered three hundred and seventy-eight while Xerxes had a thousand sail. Victory rested with the few, and Themistocles conquered in the famous battle of Salamis.

He received great honor. The Spartans took him to their city, crowned him with olive, gave him a fine chariot, and, with three hundred soldiers on horses, escorted him to the borders of the state. When he went to the Olympic games all the people rose to show him respect and honor. He was for a time the glory and pride of Athens.

But after a while the people turned against him. They said he was a traitor and the courts condemned him to death. He left Athens and wandered from country to country until at last he reached the palace of Artaxerxes, son of Xerxes and king of Persia.

He promised to show that king a way to crush Athens but asked for one year to think it over. Artaxerxes made him ruler over four cities, and he lived in comfort with his family.

His promise to Artaxerxes was never kept. Before the year was ended Themistocles died, being sixty-five years old.

CHAPTER XLVI

THE SEVEN WISE MEN

THE Greeks loved beauty, and that made them artists. They loved power, and that made them warriors. They loved wisdom, and that made them philosophers.

Many wise men, or philosophers, lived in Greece at different times. There were seven who were thought to be wiser than all the rest. After they were dead a saying of each was painted on the walls of the temple at Delphi.

These men were Pittacus, Periander, Cleobulus, Solon, the lawgiver of Athens, Chilo, Thales, and Bias of Ionia.

Pittacus was elected by the people of Mitylene to be their ruler. When he had brought order into the state and everything was peaceful and happy he gave up his office as willingly as he had taken it. We are told that he said, "The greatest blessing which a man can enjoy is the power of doing good"; "The wisest man is he who foresees the approach of misfortune"; "Victory should never be stained by blood"; and, "Pardon often does more good than punishment." His golden saying painted on the wall at Delphi was, "Take time by the forelock."

Periander, ruler of Corinth, is said to have been a harsh and cruel man. An old story says that soon after he became ruler he sent to another prince to inquire how best to keep his power. The prince said to the messenger, "Come with me!" They went together into a field of grain, and wherever they saw a tall stalk the prince struck at it and cut it down. The messenger went home and told this to Periander who said, "So will I deal with the powerful nobles of my kingdom." This story may not be true, but it shows what was thought of his way of governing. Nevertheless under his rule Corinth grew rich and strong and Periander was counted among the seven wise men. His golden saying was, "Industry conquers everything."

We already know the history of Solon, called the "lawgiver of Athens." His golden saying was, "Know thyself."

We know little of Cleobulus except that he ruled over Lindus in the island of Rhodes and that this saying of his was on the walls of the Delphian temple: "Avoid extremes"; or, as it is sometimes given, "Choose the wise middle course."

Chilo lived in Sparta and his daughter was married to the Spartan king Demaratus. His wise saying was, "Consider the end!"

Thales, born at Miletus, was a famous philosopher. He believed that water was the beginning and the ending of everything. He said, "Surety for another is ruin to yourself."

Bias was the last of the Seven Sages. He is said to have been in a storm on a vessel with a drunken crew, who, being frightened, began to pray. Bias told them, "You would better keep still, or the gods will find out that you are at sea." His golden saying is a sorrowful one: "Most men are bad!"

There was another man, probably as wise as any of the seven, though he was not counted among them. This was Pythagoras, who was born on the island of Samos but who traveled far into the East. He came back to his native place in 450 B.C., but not feeling happy there went to Crotona in Italy where he opened a school of philosophy.

He was always trying to learn something new and he found out many strange things. He discovered chords in music; that is, he learned that striking certain notes together will give a pleasing sound. That made him think that the planets as they moved through the sky, struck upon the ether in which they rolled and so made music, loud or soft, deep or shrill, according to their size, swiftness, and distance from each other. This was called the "music of the spheres," which could not be heard by those living upon the earth.

That was only a fancy, but he found out a good many truths about the planets and the stars.

A pupil asked him, "What is God?"

He answered, "God is a Mind."

"Where does He live?" inquired the pupil.

"Everywhere," replied Pythagoras.

"When did He begin to be?" inquired the other. "He never began and He will never end," returned the philosopher.

"Can he feel pain?"

"No. Only the imperfect can feel pain, and He is perfect."

"Can any man see this perfect and eternal Mind?"

"No. He is invisible. You can hardly look at the bright sun; but God is so much brighter that no one can see Him with the eye; although He can be known by our minds. He is true, holy, and unchangeable; and from Him come the life and motion of whatever lives and moves."

Pythagoras taught that the soul lives forever but at death passes from one body into another, dwelling sometimes in a man, sometimes in an animal. He declared that he remembered having lived several times as different creatures.

Once he saw a man beating a dog which yelped and cried.

He said, "You are cruel. Stop beating that dog!"

The other answered, "Why should I stop? It is my dog."

PYTHAGORAS AND HIS FRIEND

"Do you not hear him cry?" asked the wise man.

"Yes; I hear him plainly. What then?" replied the owner of the beast.

"Poor ignorant man!" said the philosopher. "In that dog's cry I hear the voice of a dear friend of mine who died a number of years ago. He has been born again in the body of this poor dog. Treat him well for my sake."

CHAPTER XLVII

THE RICHEST KING

NEARLY six hundred years before the Christian era began, Crœsus was king of Lydia. He was a brave and successful warrior and had a large kingdom. He was at that time the richest man in the world, though his fortune of nine millions of dollars would not now be considered very great. He was also extremely proud of his wealth.

It is said that when Solon was upon his travels he went to Sardis, the capital city of Lydia. The king was glad to see him and showed him all the treasures gathered in his palace. There were chests full of gold and silver money, boxes in which shone thousands of precious stones, rooms in which hung many dresses of silk, velvet, and cloth of gold. There were pictures, statues, ivory carvings, shields, swords, spears, and musical instruments, gathered from every part of the known world.

Solon had never seen such treasures but he did not say, "How wonderful! How beautiful!"

Crœsus was not pleased at this silence. "Did

you ever see a happier man than I am?" he inquired at last.

"Yes," said Solon.

"Who was he, and where did he live?" asked the king.

"He lived in Athens, and his name was Tellus. He always had enough to live on, and when he died it was in battle fighting for his country. Not only his children but the state mourned for him. I never knew anybody else so happy as he."

"Who was next in happiness?" asked Crœsus.

"Two sons of a priestess of Hera in Argos. Once she was to offer sacrifice and the oxen which should draw her were not ready. Her sons harnessed themselves to the chariot and brought her to the temple. She prayed that those dutiful sons might receive the best of all gifts, and her prayer was answered. That night they fell asleep and never woke again. They passed away without sorrow or pain. Their kindred loved them, their country honored them. Who could be happier than they?"

"Do you mean that a rich and powerful king is not happy?" asked the king angrily.

"O king!" replied the sage, we can call no man truly happy until he dies. Power, health, and riches may all pass away. That which we may lose in a day cannot make us happy and he who looks for joy in such things is not wise."

Crœsus was displeased with these words of Solon but he could not forget them. He was not really so happy as he pretended to be. He had two sons, one of them dumb; the other, Atys, handsome and gifted. Crœsus dreamed that this son was killed by an instrument with an iron point. He was much afraid that the dream would come true.

Gordius, king of Phrygia, had two sons one of whom, Adrastus, accidentally killed the other. His father drove the unfortunate boy from his court; and he went to Crœsus who received him kindly.

A wild boar had done much damage in the fields and vineyards, and Crœsus sent Atys with Adrastus to hunt and kill the beast. They found him and Adrastus threw an iron-pointed spear, which missed the animal and struck Atys in the side. Thus the prophecy of the dream was fulfilled.

It is said that, some time after, the son who was dumb saw his father in danger of being killed. The power of speech came to him and he called out, "Look, father! Take care, take care!"

Cyrus was now gaining power and Crœsus, afraid for his kingdom, asked for help from the Greeks and advice from their oracles. All gave him fine words, but none kept the promise.

Crœsus led out his own army against Cyrus, and fought a battle in which neither side won the victory. Croesus retreated toward Sardis and Cyrus followed. The Lydian king ordered his cavalry to charge upon the Persians. Cyrus put a number of camels in the front rank, and when the horses saw those strange beasts nothing could hold them. They ran wildly away and the defeat of Crœsus was complete.

He shut himself up in his city of Sardis which Cyrus besieged for many months. One day a soldier, leaning over the wall of the citadel, dropped his helmet which rolled into the plain below. He climbed after it down the face of the rock and went up again by the same path.

A soldier in the army of Cyrus saw this and asked permission to lead a party up the rocky height. They started in the night. The Lydians did not watch that point for they did not think an enemy would come that way. The Persians took the citadel by surprise and quickly had the city at their mercy.

Crœsus was taken prisoner and Cyrus ordered him to be burned alive as a sacrifice to the gods.

He was chained and laid upon the piled up wood. As the fire was kindled he called out in a loud voice, "O Solon! Solon! Solon!"

Cyrus ordered that the fire should be put out and the captive brought before him.

"Upon whom did you call so earnestly?" he asked. "Was it your god to whom you prayed, or was it some friend whom you remembered?"

"O king!" said the captive Crœsus, "it was the name of a wise man who warned me that I could not be happy while I trusted in power, health, or riches.

"My power is gone for I am your slave. My riches are mine no more for they are yours. What health have

THE CAPTURE OF THE CITADEL

I, who a moment ago was at the door of death and in another moment may return there by your command? I am the most unhappy wretch in all the world!"

But Cyrus said, "I will give you freedom, and you shall be my friend." Often afterwards he took the advice of the man whom Solon had warned.

Of this story only part can be true. Solon had gone home to Athens before Crœsus began to reign. But it is true that Crœsus was thought to be the richest man in the world; that he had two sons one of whom was deaf and dumb; that the other son was killed by accident; that Crœsus was defeated by Cyrus, and ordered to be burned alive; and that he was spared, and became the friend of his conqueror.

CHAPTER XLVIII

GLORIOUS DAYS

PERICLES was the greatest statesman Athens ever had. When he was a boy he was timid and shy, afraid to talk before strangers. But when he grew up and went to battle no man was braver.

He had an excellent education. Music and philosophy were his favorite studies. Most of all he loved oratory, the art of public speaking. He spoke with such force and energy that he was said to thunder and lighten.

Although he was good looking his head was of such a strange shape that he was called "peaked head."

While yet a very young man he began to take an interest in politics, placing himself on the side of the poor rather than of the rich. For about forty years he was a leader. In all that time he was never seen in the streets except on his way to the senate or public meetings. He was too busy to idle about the market place, hearing and telling news like most of the Athenians. He never went to feasts and had only a few close friends. Because he was not rich enough to grant the citizens many gifts he used the public money to amuse and feed them. By his orders every citizen of Athens received the price of a theater ticket whenever a play was given. Every soldier and every citizen who served in the courts was paid. He had grand gardens laid out for public use, and in the time of his greatest power he caused the most beautiful buildings in the world to be erected on the Acropolis, the highest point of the city.

He thought all the Greek states ought to unite and help one another. A congress was called at Athens to consider about rebuilding the temples which the Persians had destroyed, and to arrange that any Greek ship should sail, free of cost or danger, into and out of any Greek port. This was a wise and excellent plan, but it could not be carried out because Sparta was jealous and would not agree to it.

The Phocians attacked the temple at Delphi and seized its treasures. The Spartans drove away the Phocians and, as a reward, were given the first right to consult the oracle. When the Spartans were gone home Pericles went to Delphi, put the Phocians again in power, and took for Athens the right which Sparta had gained.

In time of great danger he paid one enemy to march away. Then with fifty vessels and fifty thousand men he fought and defeated other foes.

He paid much attention to the navy. Every year he had sixty galleys sent out for a cruise of eight months, so that their crews might be well trained in the management of vessels. No other state of Greece had so many ships or such good sailors.

Through his wisdom and courage, peace and prosperity were given to Athens. He built the Long Walls which joined the city to its seaport, Piræus. They were sixty feet high and more than four miles in length.

In the war with Sparta he advised the country people to bring their goods inside these walls so that they might be safe from their enemies.

He made the people feel that they were great and powerful and need not be afraid of any foe. They were always ready for war, yet well satisfied to be at peace. He caused the treasures of the united cities to be brought from Delos to Athens, and used them freely in making that city stronger and more splendid.

Under his care the arts flourished. There were many more fine buildings and statues in Athens than ever before. He built a theater called the Odeon, where musical festivals were to be held. The Parthenon, erected by his orders, was the grandest temple ever raised by human hands. When some persons blamed him for using so much of the public money he answered, "Very well. The buildings must be put up but my name shall be placed upon them instead of yours." The crowd answered, "Spend all the money you choose."

Sparta was jealous and angry at this splendor and made war on Athens. At the same time the plague, a dreadful sickness of which people died in a few hours, broke out in the crowded city. For this Pericles was blamed and fined, yet he was elected one of the generals for the next year. His son, a sister, and his most intimate friends died of the disease. When his second son died the heart of Pericles seemed broken. As he placed the funeral garland on the young man's head the father burst into tears.

Shortly afterwards he also died. While he was sick and his friends around him were telling what good he had done he said, "Do not forget that I never caused any Athenian to put on mourning."

When his property was settled it was found that he had never kept or used for himself a penny of the public money. Athens built his tomb and set up a statue in his memory. She saw her brightest glory in the days of Pericles.

CHAPTER XLIX

THE WISE MAN WITH
THE SNUB NOSE

NEARLY five hundred years before the Christian era, Socrates was born in a village near Athens. His father was a sculptor,—that is, a man who carved marble images,—and this boy was brought up to the same trade. A group of the Three Graces in the Acropolis was said to have been made by him.

He was not highly educated, although as a boy he went to the public schools and was a faithful scholar. But he was a deep thinker and as he grew up he listened to the teaching of wise men whenever he could. He was not satisfied. "They are not wise enough for me," he said. "I must try to be wiser than they are."

Every young man was expected to go to war and fight for his country. Socrates did his duty as a soldier and was faithful there as everywhere.

He married a woman named Xanthippe. She may have been pleasant and agreeable at first, but afterwards she became an ill-tempered scold. One reason for this was that Socrates gave up work so that he could go about teaching people truth and goodness. Other men gained their living by teaching; but Socrates made no charge, had no regular school, and gave no regular lectures. He went into the markets, the gymnasium, and the work-shops, and talked to people wherever he met them. He did not say, "It is very warm to-day," or, "I think it will rain before night," or; "What is the latest news?" or, "Did you hear about that robbery last night?"

He asked instead questions such as these: "What is truth?" or, "Did you ever see your own soul?" or, "How do you suppose the gods would be treated if they came into this market place?"

He never claimed to know anything, but was always asking other people what they knew, and how they could prove it to be true. This made many people angry, and they hooted after him and threw mud at him in the streets. Still he had numerous friends, and though he would take no regular pay they made him presents so that his wife and children should not starve.

Xanthippe was cross and angry because they were so poor. When her husband came in at night she would say to him, "Here you come! Here you come! All day you have been with that conceited Alcibiades and your other rich friends in the market place, while the children and I perish with hunger. What have you brought home? Nothing; not a penny, not a crust of bread! You have eaten, no doubt; you have had bread and figs and olives while we have fed on air. Such a man to be a husband and father! No wonder the boys

AN ARGUMENT WITH SOCRATES

pelt you with stones and mud! No wonder they shout, 'Madman,' after you."

Socrates never answered. He expected to be poor and did not expect to be happy. To be good and truly wise and to help others to goodness and wisdom was all he desired or cared for. That was his work and in that he found joy.

A man who told men's characters by looking at their faces went to Athens. Some friends of Socrates took him to that teacher who had never met the sage. He saw before him a man very poorly dressed, with a large, bald head, coarse features, thick lips, and a snub nose. He said, "This man is selfish, false, unjust, very fond of pleasure, and does not care who suffers so that he has his own way."

His friends cried out, "No! That is not true. This is Socrates, the best man in Greece!"

Socrates said, "The teacher is right. By nature I am all that he has said. I am only different because I have conquered myself, compelling myself to do right instead of wrong."

He claimed that a spirit went always with him, telling him what was right. Sometimes he would not speak for a long time and when his friends asked, "Why are you so silent, Socrates?" he answered, "I am listening to the divine voice within me." He declared that he always obeyed that voice.

His questions which led people on until they showed their ignorance caused many persons to hate him. It was said that he wanted to bring in new gods; that he would do anything to make money; that he taught the young to despise parents and relatives and to disobey the laws; and that he encouraged the rich to take advantage of the poor. All this was false but he was arrested and brought before the courts. They ordered him not to teach any more but he said he would rather die. It was then ordered that he should drink hemlock, a fatal poison.

In prison he quietly sat and talked with his friends. One of them said, "I cannot bear to see you die, innocent of any crime." He answered, "Would it please you if I died guilty?" He believed that his soul would never die although his body was to be killed.

When the hour of sunset came he drank the cup of poison. In a few minutes he was dead. Athens had sent away forever one of her best and greatest citizens.

CHAPTER L

A WASTED LIFE

ONE of the handsomest, bravest, richest, and most talented young men of Athens was Alcibiades. When he was five years old his father was killed in battle. The men who brought up the boy allowed him to have his own way in everything, so that he grew to be very stubborn and selfish.

One day he was playing in the street when a chariot came driving up.

"Stop!" said Alcibiades to the driver. "You shall not pass this way. Stop, I tell you!"

"Who are you?" replied the driver. "By what right do you stop me? I shall certainly pass this way."

The boy threw himself in front of the wheel of the chariot. "Now drive on if you dare!" he cried. "Drive over my body and see what will happen to you!"

Of course the driver had to stop but Alcibiades was much to blame for such behavior.

He was wrestling with a playmate and was likely

to be thrown. He bit the boy, who said, "O Alcibiades, that is not fair! You bite like a woman."

"No," he answered, "I bite like a lion!"

When he was eighteen years old his fortune was given into his own hands. He spent much money on dress, and even his iron shield was inlaid with gold and ivory. The young men of Athens tried to be like him. He spoke with a lisp; so did they. They combed their hair as he combed his, and wore clothes like those he wore. They drank and gambled with him and were proud when people said, "There go the friends of Alcibiades."

But with all his faults he was not idle. He studied oratory and philosophy that he might be able to speak well and reason rightly. One of his teachers was the wise Socrates, who tried to help him to be good. He liked the philosopher and while under his care behaved very well. They went to war side by side and in one of the battles Alcibiades was wounded. Then Socrates stood over him and kept away his enemies until help came and carried the wounded youth to a place of safety.

At another time Socrates with his troop was running from the enemy and was in great danger. But Alcibiades, who was on horseback, rode down those foes and saved his friend.

In the company of the wise and good this young man seemed to be like them, but with companions of his own age he was the leader in everything wrong and wicked.

He delighted in sports. Once he took seven

chariots to the Olympic games and put them all into the races. With them he won the first, second, and fourth prizes.

Because he spent his money freely and provided amusement for the people he was very popular. He spoke in the public meetings, fought in the army, and was a leading citizen before he was thirty years old.

He was greatly in favor of a war against Sicily, by which he thought the glory and power of Athens would be much increased. A fleet was made ready and was about to sail with him as leader when a strange thing happened.

In Athens, at the crossings of the larger streets, busts of the god Hermes had been set up. One morning it was found that nearly every one of these was injured. From some the heads had been broken off, from others the noses or the ears had been knocked away. The people were frightened and angry. The god and the city had been insulted. The cry was raised that this was the work of Alcibiades and his drunken young companions. Yet in the midst of this outcry the fleet sailed with him as one of its commanders.

His enemies at home said he must be called back to answer for his crime. He escaped from the fleet, went to Sparta, told the plans of the Athenians, and did all he could to help the enemies of his native city.

Although absent from Athens he was tried there, found guilty of treason and sentenced to death. The state took all his property and the priests solemnly cursed him in their temples.

He lived at Sparta for several years and seemed like one of the people of that land. He dressed plainly, ate coarse food, exercised every day in the gymnasium, and gave the rulers good and helpful advice. But some persons did not trust him and he heard that the king of Sparta had ordered him to be put to death. He fled to the camp of Tissaphernes, a Persian general. There he made himself so agreeable that the Persian was never happy without him.

After a while the Athenian army passed a vote that Alcibiades should be pardoned and recalled and made one of their generals. He was invited to return, was made a leader, and by his help several victories were gained.

The records of his banishment were then sunk in the sea, his property was given back to him, he was blessed in those temples where he had been cursed; and all the forces, by land and sea, were placed under his command.

In the very next battle he was defeated. He was disgraced and could no longer be leader. He fled to his castle in Thrace, hired soldiers, made war on the Thracians, and helped the Greek cities.

Persia, Sparta, and Athens agreed together that he must die. He had gone to the house of a friend, a woman named Timandra. Soldiers who had been sent against him surrounded the house and set it on fire. He rushed out with his sword in his hand but he was shot with many arrows, and fell to rise no more.

Timandra gave him honorable burial but at the

funeral she was the only mourner. He had been false to himself and to everybody else, and nobody was sorry when he died, not yet forty years old.

CHAPTER LI

THE RETREAT OF THE TEN THOUSAND

A MONG the pupils of Socrates was a young man named Xenophon. He went to Sardis and enlisted in the army of Cyrus the Younger. This prince intended to take the throne of Persia from his brother Artaxerxes. He deceived his soldiers by telling them that he was raising his army to fight the Pisidians. He led them against his brother, but was defeated and killed near Cunaxa, a city in the province of Babylon.

Besides his own troops, Cyrus had gathered a force of ten thousand Greeks, who now found themselves nearly fifteen hundred miles from home, in a strange country with enemies all around them.

Artaxerxes sent a messenger who ordered the Greeks to lay down their arms. They answered, "If the king thinks he is strong enough let him come and take them."

Ariæus had taken command of the army of Cyrus. The Greek leaders wished him to claim the Persian crown and offered to fight for him, but he answered that he meant to retreat and that if the Greeks were going with him they must join him that night. This they did and the retreat of the army began. The next day Artaxerxes sent word that he was willing to make peace on equal terms. Clearchus, the Greek leader, said, "Tell your king that we must first fight with him, for we have had no breakfast and no man can talk about peace to the Greeks until they have been fed." The king sent guides to lead these men to villages where they found plenty of food.

Tissaphernes, a Persian general and friend of Artaxerxes, now came to them and offered to lead them back to Greece. They agreed and began the journey. The Persians under Ariæus and those led by Tissaphernes were united in one army. They marched three miles ahead of the Greeks, who kept together following their own leaders. After a march of twenty days the armies halted. There had been some trouble between the Greeks and Persians, and Clearchus asked to see Tissaphernes so that an agreement might be reached. The Persian leader declared that he was friendly toward the Greeks and invited Clearchus and four other generals to visit him the next day. When they entered the Persian camp they were seized, put in irons, and sent to the court of Artaxerxes where they were soon afterwards put to death.

The Greeks were left without leaders. Xenophon, though young, was wise and brave. He called the captains together and said, "Do not give up to these barbarians; rather let us trust to our courage and skill in war and try to fight our way home." The soldiers cheered and chose Xenophon and four others to be their generals and to lead them back to Greece. Then they began their march which was to be one long battle.

At first they formed a hollow square of the heavily armed men, and in the center they put the baggage, the cattle, and the lighter armed soldiers, as well as some women and children who were with them.

Before starting they burned most of their wagons, all their tents and much of their baggage. Then they ate their breakfast and moved forward.

The enemy followed them with horse soldiers and a large company of men with arrows and slings. The Greeks found their own bows would not shoot far enough to do any harm. They sent soldiers to drive away the Persians, who ran and rode so fast that the Greeks could not come near them.

Xenophon found among the Greeks some Rhodians who could use the sling, and formed them into a company. He took as many horses as could be spared from the baggage carts and put soldiers upon them. In this way he had fifty horsemen and two hundred slingers.

When the enemy attacked on the next day these Greeks blew their trumpets and charged. The Persians ran away. This happened day after day.

Xenophon then divided all his soldiers into companies of a hundred men, each company under a captain. This was better than the hollow square, which was either broken up or badly crowded in going through narrow places.

Almost every night they camped in villages where they found plenty to eat. The Persians followed them shooting arrows and slinging stones but not doing much harm. When the Greeks reached large villages they rested several days and took care of the wounded.

In one of the marches up a mountain side, Xenophon said, "Forward, men! Up, up!"

A soldier complained, "It is very well for you to say that. You are on horseback but I can hardly drag my shield."

The general jumped down, took the man's shield from him, pushed him out of the ranks, and marched with the soldiers. The grumbler was pelted with stones until he was glad to beg Xenophon to give him the shield and mount his horse again.

They came to rivers so deep that they were forced to march many miles to find a place to cross. Mountains were climbed with the enemy rolling down huge rocks which broke the legs or ribs of those whom they struck.

In the highlands of Armenia a great snowstorm came on and the ground was covered to a depth of six feet. Many cattle and prisoners and thirty soldiers died. Some lost their eyesight; others had their feet frozen so that they could not walk. It was a time of dreadful

"THE SEA! THE SEA!"

suffering, but all who were able marched on for that was the only way of escape.

At last they reached a country where the king gave them a guide who promised to show them the sea. Day after day he led them up among the mountains until they reached a very high point. The first who climbed it raised a great shout and officers and men hurried from every side. There far away, sparkling in the sunshine, lay the blue water. "The Sea! The Sea!" they cried. Tears were in their eyes, brave soldiers though they were. They shook hands and hugged each other in their delight.

Marching down from the mountains they reached, after some days, Trebizond, a Greek city on the Black Sea.

They stayed there thirty days, resting and holding games and sacrificing to their gods. They ran, they wrestled, they boxed, they raced horses down the hills and up again.

They could not find ships enough for all, but on those they did get they put the sick and weak, while the stronger marched by land and at last they reached home.

Eight thousand six hundred were left of the ten thousand. They had been a year and three months on that long journey from distant Babylon to their own land.

War was their trade and they could not be happy at anything else. So most of them enlisted under a general who was making war for Sparta against the Persians. They thus had the satisfaction of again fighting their old enemies.

Xenophon, who lived to be a very old man, wrote the history of the retreat from Persia. He was also the author of other interesting books, in one of which he has given us his recollections of his famous teacher Socrates.

CHAPTER LII

FALSE AND CRUEL

SPARTA found her greatest though not her best citizen in Lysander. He was born a Helot,—that is, a slave,—but he was given a good Spartan education and by his own efforts gained the rights of a citizen. He was a very cunning man and cared nothing for truth or honor. He said that where courage was not enough deceit must be used; that the fox is wiser and more successful than the lion; that oaths are made to deceive men, and only foolish people keep them. He was willing to work hard and to suffer many things, but he loved nobody and cared only for himself and his own power and glory.

He hated Athens and wished to humble her. Cyrus the Younger was at war with that city and the Spartans were helping him. Lysander was made commander of the fleet. There were no ships and he had much trouble in getting together seventy sail. He took these to the harbor of Ephesus. That city had never been friendly to Athens, and in its port he was nearer to the Persians. Cyrus gave him money so that he could pay higher wages to the sailors and many went to him from the Athenian ships.

Alcibiades, who led the Athenians, blockaded Lysander in the harbor of Ephesus and went away, leaving Antiochus in charge. Lysander made a sudden attack, sank Antiochus and his ship, and took or destroyed fifteen vessels.

Admirals were only elected for a certain time and could not be re-elected. When Lysander's time was out he was made vice admiral and remained the real leader of the fleet. He went back to Ephesus and built more ships. Cyrus gave him plenty of money to pay soldiers and sailors, invited him to Sardis, and went away on a journey to Media leaving Lysander to rule in his place.

In the spring he was ready for battle. He sailed about the sea in every direction, landed at different places to show that he could do as he pleased, and at last took his fleet to the Hellespont. He attacked the city of Lampsacus and captured it with all its money and supplies.

The Athenian ships were gathered in an open bay opposite Lampsacus and near the mouth of Goat River. No town was near and every day the sailors had to go a mile inland to get something to eat. This was done for four days and daily the Athenian sailors grew more careless. On the fifth day, when they had gone inland and not many were left with the ships, Lysander sailed down the bay and attacked the fleet. The few men who had remained by the ships were not enough to work them and all except eight vessels surrendered to Lysander. These put out to sea under the command of Conon and escaped. Lysander captured one hundred and eighty ships and took three thousand prisoners, whom he treated with the most savage cruelty.

He conquered a number of other places but allowed the Athenians who were living in them to go back to their own city. He wished to crowd Athens so that there would be more mouths to feed when he made his attack there.

Troops were ordered to surround that unhappy capital by land. Lysander with two hundred ships sailed to the mouth of the Piræus and blockaded the port. Food became very scarce in the city, though a few vessels sailed through the enemy's fleet and brought in grain. The citizens met and agreed to give up to Sparta all they owned in other places, keeping only the Piræus and the Walls.

This word was carried to Sparta. A message was sent back that the walls of the harbor and those joining it to the city must be torn down; that all the ships of war except twelve must be given up to the Spartans; that troops must be sent to their help whenever called for; and that Athens could rule only in Attica.

Athens was obliged to yield. Lysander had the harbor filled up and the Long Walls pulled down. While that was going on he ordered the most joyful music to be played, to mock the grief of the Athenians.

He took away the power from the people and put thirty Spartan captains in charge of the city. These were called the "Thirty Tyrants." Athens was no longer the beautiful mistress of Greece; she was the poor slave of Sparta.

Lysander carried back the rich spoils of war to Sparta, and put them in the public treasury.

He was very vain and proud and hired poets to write his praises and musicians to sing them. He was the first Greek to whom altars were built and sacrifices offered as if he had been a god. He went to war against the Thebans and was killed in battle. Divine honors could not preserve him from the universal fate of mankind.

CHAPTER LIII

THE THEBAN PAIR

ALTHOUGH less important in many ways than other cities of Greece, Thebes had been quietly growing in strength and influence. She was at peace with the other states when a Spartan army, marching through her territory, seized the citadel and took possession of the city. Sparta held this advantage during four years. Then the people of Thebes rose, captured the citadel and drove out the Spartan soldiers.

The two leaders of this attack were Pelopidas and Epaminondas, who were called the Theban Pair. Epaminondas was the greater of the two. He was the son of a poor family but he had a good education and a noble character. He did not care to be rich. The one thing for which he lived was to do right and to help his native city. He was quiet in manner, amiable in disposition, sincere in heart, and wise in judgment. He was considered almost perfect,—one of the greatest and perhaps the best of all the Greeks.

Pelopidas laid the plan for capturing the citadel. He gathered a company of young men and dressed them like dancing-girls, but under their fanciful garments each man wore a sword. They were to go to the citadel on a night when the Spartan general gave a feast, and to ask general admittance to share and help in the enjoyment.

On the morning before the feast some one sent a letter to the general telling him of the plan. He did not read it but said, "To-day is for pleasure; to-morrow we will attend to business."

Night came and the soldiers in the citadel were very gay. A knock was heard at the gates. A soldier said, "General, a company of dancing-women ask to come in that they may show their art and share our joy."

"On this night," said the general, "all the world is welcome. Let them enter and dance before us."

The gates were thrown open. Pelopidas and his party entered. They danced a very little while; then at a word from the leader drew their swords and rushed upon the soldiers. The first man to fall was the foolish general who had said, "Pleasure to-day; business to-morrow."

The citadel was taken from the Spartans and Thebes was again free.

When Epaminondas and his friend had rescued Thebes from the Spartans, they tried to show their fellow-citizens that virtue and liberty are the best things.

"To be free," said Epaminondas, "is most to be desired but the false and wicked are never free. The man who conquers himself has liberty; all others are really slaves. Why do you spend your money for rich food

DISGUISED AS DANCING GIRLS

and expensive wines when those who eat simply have the best health and he who drinks water can never be drunken? You look for pleasure, but in the wrong way. True pleasure is found in living plainly and in doing right."

Thebes became a leading city. A convention of the Greek states was held at Sparta to arrange for a general peace. Epaminondas was so independent that the king of Sparta was angry and declared war against Thebes.

Twenty days later the two armies met on the plain of Leuctra and a fierce battle was fought. Here Epaminondas proved himself to be a great general and the Spartans were severely beaten. They were surprised and ashamed at this defeat for they had considered the Thebans dull and slow. But the Spartans were no longer so warlike as they had been and the Thebans had improved in war with Epaminondas for their leader.

He marched into Laconia up to the very gates of Sparta but did not attack the city. He burned the crops and villages in the valley of the river Eurotas and then led his troops homeward.

For two following years armies went out from Thebes and fought against the Spartans. In a battle in Thessaly, Pelopidas was killed. At Mantinea, Epaminondas won another victory over the men of Sparta. But it was his last battle. A dart thrown by a Spartan entered his breast and went nearly through his body. He fell to the ground insensible.

His friends bent over him, full of sorrow, for they

saw that nothing could be done to help him. After a while he opened his eyes.

"Where is my shield?" he asked, for if a soldier lost his shield he was disgraced.

"It is here, general," they said. "Let me see it," he demanded, and they brought it to him. "How goes the fight?" he inquired.

"The enemy are defeated," was the answer. "We have won the day and hold the field!"

"Then all is well," he said. "Pull out the dart!"

"General," they replied, "we dare not."

"Do you mean that when the dart is drawn I must die?" he asked.

"Yes," they said sorrowfully.

With his own hand he drew out the weapon and the blood gushed forth.

"He dies," they cried. "He dies, and leaves no child to carry on his name."

"I do not die," he answered. "I begin to live, and I have two daughters. They are named Leuctra and Mantinea, and while they are remembered I shall not be forgotten!"

CHAPTER LIV

PHILIP OF MACEDON

MACEDON, or Macedonia, was a mountainous country lying north of Greece. Its people were not Greeks but their kings claimed to be of the same stock as the Hellenes. One of those kings built roads, erected forts, improved his army, and tried to interest his people in literature and art. He paid Zeuxis, the great artist, to paint beautiful pictures on the inner walls of his palace. Euripides, the famous poet, visited this king, and died at his capital city.

The greatest of all these kings was Philip. When his father died and left him the kingdom he was twenty-four years old, tall and good-looking, with pleasant manners and a kindly nature. But he was not truthful, and would use any means to gain his purpose.

When he was a boy he lived for a while at Thebes in Greece. It is likely that he knew Plato, and it is sure that he had trained himself to be one of the best speakers of the time. He learned from the Thebans many lessons in the art of war, and afterwards introduced into his own army the Greek phalanx. This was a company of soldiers with sixteen men in front and sixteen men deep.

Each of these carried a long spear extending eighteen feet before and six feet behind him. Horses could not be driven against those spears and foot-soldiers could not reach the men who carried them.

Philip was very ambitious, very determined, and a good judge of men. Where he could not conquer he bought; and he declared that he had taken more towns with silver than with iron.

Another man wished to be king and Athens favored him. A battle was fought and Philip won. He took some Athenians prisoners, but set them free, gave them handsome presents and offered to be a friend to Athens. The Athenians made peace with him as he desired.

He then turned to his other enemies, fought one after another and defeated all. In one year's time his kingdom was free and quiet.

Other wars soon broke out and he had just taken a city when three men came running to him one after another.

The first one said, "O king, your horses have won a race at the Olympic games!"

The second cried out, "O king, your general has defeated the Illyrians!"

The third one shouted, "O king, in your palace at home a noble son is born!"

The king was very proud and happy at all this good news.

He captured another city, sent people to live in it, and called it Philippi after himself. With this city he obtained some gold mines which made him richer than he had ever been.

While he was leading the attack upon another town, an arrow shot from the wall put out one of his eyes. When the town fell into his power he left the inhabitants one garment each, and set them free to go where they would; but he pulled down every house in the place, and sent other people of his own to build and live there.

In one of his wars he was beaten and retreated into Macedonia. There he gathered more soldiers and gave each a crown of laurel. The laurel was the favorite tree of Apollo, and Philip said, "My soldiers and I are warriors of the sun god, and he will take care of us."

The very next battle made him master of Thessaly.

Demosthenes, the orator of Athens, saw the danger to that city from this ambitious man and began to deliver speeches against Philip. The Macedonian king went on with his plans, and when he had taken another city he not only threw down the houses but sold the people as slaves.

The Athenians tried to unite the other states against him, but Philip sent them word that he was willing to make peace. Athens sent ten men to make a treaty, one of them being Demosthenes. The king trifled with them and put them off day after day, but at last persuaded them to march with him into Thessaly.

Finally he became master of all Greece.

To Athens he was kind and favorable but he treated Thebes differently. He put a number of soldiers into the citadel and ruled the city as he pleased.

A congress was held at Corinth and the Greeks agreed to make war on Persia and to elect Philip leader of their armies. Only the Spartans refused to consent. To punish them he took away part of their lands which he gave to other people.

While he was getting ready to go to Persia he gave a grand wedding feast for his daughter. The Greeks sent him golden crowns as presents. On the second day of the festival there was a splendid procession in which men carried images of the Olympian gods. With them a statue of Philip was carried as if he also were a god.

Dressed in white he marched between his son and the bridegroom. The guards were kept at a distance to show that the king trusted the people. A young man rushed forward and stabbed him with a short sword. The feast was broken up. Philip was dead, and his son, Alexander, stood ready to take his father's place.

CHAPTER LV

THE MAN WITH THE
SILVER TONGUE

THE greatest orator the world ever knew was probably Demosthenes. His father made knives and swords at Athens, and in that city Demosthenes was born. He was a delicate child and had a weak voice, but he was determined to be a great public speaker.

Because he stammered, he put pebbles in his mouth, that he might learn to speak more slowly. Because his breath was short, he practiced running uphill to make himself long-winded. Knowing that his voice was weak, he went down to the seashore and shouted against the roaring waves, so that when the people were noisy in public meetings he could make himself heard. He even built a study entirely underground and practiced speaking there, so that he might gain a loud, clear voice.

He was a pupil in the school of Plato and learned much from that wise teacher.

When he was seven years old his father died. The

men who were left in charge of his property cheated him. He said nothing until he was eighteen years old. Then he went into the courts of law and accused his guardians of dishonesty and wrong. He made five orations on that subject and won his case, but could never get back all his money.

That he might learn a good style in writing he copied the history of Thucydides several times. To acquire a good manner of speaking he tried to imitate Pericles. When he began to appear in public a man said, "Your arguments smell of the lamp," which meant that they had been carefully studied by night.

"Yes," replied Demosthenes, "but your lamp and mine are used for different purposes." He meant that while he studied the other was carousing.

He took up the profession of a lawyer, but his finest speeches were political addresses against the evils of the time.

Philip of Macedon was then growing more and more powerful. Demosthenes was determined to hinder him from mastering Athens. In twelve years he delivered eleven orations against Philip, several of which were especially called Philippics because they were so full of sharp and bitter words against the Macedonian king. He went to other cities and persuaded them to unite against Philip, who, he said, would conquer all unless all combined against him.

He never was chosen for any great office and never led any armies. He was in the battle of Chæronea fighting against Philip; but it is said that he threw away his shield and fled from the field. Yet no man was more highly honored by the state. It was proposed that the city should give him a golden crown as a reward for what he had done. A prominent citizen said that such an action would not be according to law. The case was put off for six years. Demosthenes then made an address, "On the Crown," which is thought to be the best of all his speeches. It was really the history of his life. He won the case and the crown was given to him.

When Alexander became king of Macedon and thought of being a mighty conqueror, he sent word to Athens that eight of the chief orators, one of them Demosthenes, should be sent to him. A public meeting was held to talk over the matter. Demosthenes told the fable of the wolves and the sheep.

"There was once a time," he said, "when the wolves were very anxious to be at peace with the shepherds. They said they were sorry that those good men were angry at them and did not trust them. There was no cause for that feeling, as the wolves did not mean to attack the folds. For that reason they wished the shepherds would not keep dogs.

"The shepherds were pleased to find the wolves so friendly. They sent away their dogs and all was peace until a dark night came. Then while the shepherds were asleep and the sheep were helpless the wolves burst into the folds and made an end of the flock."

The people of Athens did not give up their orators but found some other way to satisfy Alexander.

Some years later Demosthenes was charged with

receiving money from the king of Persia to help the cause of that ruler. He was convicted and sentenced to pay a very large sum of money. Not intending to pay the amount, he left the city and went into exile.

As he passed out of the gate, he lifted up his hands, and said, "O Athene, goddess of these towers, why do you delight in three such monsters as the owl, the dragon, and the people?"

After the death of Alexander he was recalled to Athens and went back in honor. But the new king, Antipater, gave orders that he should be put to death. Demosthenes fled to a neighboring island and took refuge in a temple there. When he found that the soldiers of the king were following him and that he could not escape he said, "Permit me to go to the inner room and write a few lines."

He sat down and took out his pen, which he always carried with him. After writing a few words he suddenly unscrewed the top of the pen and swallowed a poison which he had hidden there. So ended the life of Demosthenes, the greatest of orators.

CHAPTER LVI

THE MAN CALLED "THE BROAD"

T HE Greeks were very fond of philosophy, which means "the love of wisdom." By this study they were trying to find out two things,—first, where the world and all things upon it came from, and secondly, what was the best and noblest way for man to live.

One of the wise men said that water was the beginning of everything. Another said that all came from fire. Still another taught that somehow everything came from the air. At last one wiser than the rest said that everything came from one great Mind, wise and strong and everlasting.

They did not all think alike as to how men ought to live. Some said, "Do everything that will make you happy." Their pupils thought that meant to eat and drink and dance and be gay.

Another school said, "Do not try to be happy but to do your duty. Do not love anybody very much, do not seek after pleasure, do not be afraid of pain. Eat simple food, wear plain clothes, be honest and faithful, wrong no one, serve your country. Do not be too eager to live, do not be afraid to die. Do right no matter what comes or goes."

These last teachers were called "Stoics," and many of their scholars were good and noble men who would rather die than do wrong.

It is hard to say which of all the philosophers was greatest, but one of the wisest was called Plato. That was not his real name. Plato means "broad," and he was called so because his shoulders, or his forehead, or both, were so broad. His real name was Aristocles.

He is said to have been born in Athens the year that Pericles died. Others say his birthplace was in the island of Ægina. He was related to Solon the lawgiver. After he had become famous as a writer and speaker it was said that, when he was a little child and asleep, bees settled on his lips to sip honey from them.

In his youth he tried many things. He ran and wrestled in the Olympic games; he wrote poetry; he studied grammar, music, and gymnastics. Nothing satisfied him until he met Socrates. Then he said, "Now I know what to do. I shall be a philosopher."

After the death of Socrates, Plato went away from Athens to Megara and spent several years in writing books. He tells much about the life and teaching and death of his old master and friend, Socrates, whom he loved and honored.

He then traveled into Egypt and Sicily and among the Greek cities in lower Italy. In Syracuse, the capital of Sicily, he became acquainted with the king, Dionysius the Elder. He tried to teach him philosophy and to make him a better man; but the king did not wish to be wise or good. It is said that in order to get rid of this troublesome teacher he sold him as a slave. When a rich friend of Plato heard of it, he bought the philosopher from his owner and set him free. We are not sure that this part of the story is true, but we know that Dionysius was not pleased with Plato.

He was away from Athens twelve years, then returned and began to teach. Near the city was a lovely garden with shady walks, which was called "the Academy," after the hero Academus. Plato taught there, but some pupils went to him in his own house. Over the door was painted, "Let no one enter here who does not know geometry."

He made no charge for teaching, but accepted presents if any one wished to give. Like Socrates, he talked much with his scholars but also delivered regular lectures. Often his pupils sat down with him to a plain common meal, in the garden. Many great men went to his school and it is said that some women attended.

After a while he went again to Syracuse, to teach philosophy to Dionysius the Younger. He was treated better than on his first visit, but did not succeed as he desired. He had hoped that the king would let him try to make Syracuse a perfect city, but he found that nobody wished to be perfect.

Going back to Athens, he gave up politics entirely but taught as before.

When he was eighty-one years old he went to a wedding, and died suddenly in the midst of the feast. He left his property to the school he had established. He had enemies as well as many friends, but Athens built monuments to his memory.

He was a great writer and a very deep thinker. He said that a true philosopher was one who understood the inner reality of things instead of seeing only the outside appearance. He taught that the soul lives forever, and advised men to find the real and true and to love that instead of following and loving the deceitful and false.

CHAPTER LVII

THE FAITHFUL FRIENDS

DIONYSIUS the Elder was a young man who enlisted and fought in the army of Syracuse. He was so brave and faithful that everybody liked and honored him, and after a while he became general of that very army in which he had been a private soldier.

That did not satisfy him; he wanted to be greater still, so by the help of the army he made himself master of the city. For thirty-eight years he was ruler, and showed himself wise and strong, though very harsh and severe.

He liked poetry and wrote poems, some of which took prizes at Athens. He invited the wise and great Plato to come and live with him at Syracuse. But the wise man's talk was too deep and solemn for Dionysius, and it is said that he sold Plato for a slave. A friend afterwards bought him and set him free.

Two men were then living in Syracuse who were firm friends. Where one was found the other could generally be seen, for they were almost always together.

One was named Damon, the other Pythias, or rather Phintias. Damon had called Dionysius a tyrant, and had tried to kill him, that the land might be free from his rule. Damon was arrested and orders were given that he should be put to death. His wife and child were then at a distance from Syracuse and he asked that he might be allowed to go and bid them farewell. His friend Pythias said, "I will stay in prison while he is gone and if he is not back at the appointed time I will die in his place."

Dionysius consented, for he thought that Damon would stay away and Pythias would be put to death, and so both these men would be out of his way. Pythias went to prison and Damon set out upon his journey.

He saw his wife and child, stayed with them a little while, then kissed them and said, "Good-by forever!"

He ordered a slave to bring his horse so that he might start on his return.

"Your horse, master?" said the trembling servant. "Did you say your horse?"

"Yes," cried Damon, "my horse, that I may hurry back to Syracuse. Why do you tremble and look so pale? Has anything happened to the horse?"

"Yes, master," replied the boy. "Something has happened; he is dead."

"Dead?" said the master, turning pale as the boy. "Then, traitor, you have killed him."

"O master," cried the lad, "I could not let you go

to die! Think of my mistress and the little boy. Stay with us! The tyrant will not follow you here."

"Murderer!" exclaimed Damon. "It is not my horse you have killed, it is my friend. O Pythias, Pythias!"

"Stay, master, stay!" pleaded the youth. His master struck him a heavy blow, crying, "Out of my way, traitor and murderer. I stay too long and Pythias will die."

Then he rushed away on foot toward Syracuse. He came to a little river which generally could be easily crossed, but it had risen into a raging torrent. He flung himself into the roaring water and struggled through to the opposite bank. Then he ran again until his strength was nearly gone. A merchant was riding easily along on a good horse.

"Friend," said Damon, "sell me your horse. I must reach Syracuse by sunset and I cannot run any farther. Sell me your horse. I will give you any price."

"No," answered the merchant. "I need my horse. It is too far for me to walk and if I go on foot robbers can easily overtake me."

"I cannot parley," cried Damon. "It is life or death for another as well as for myself. Will you sell?"

"No," replied the merchant.

Damon pulled the man from his horse, threw him a purse of money, mounted and rode at full speed toward the distant city.

Sunset of the third day had nearly come. The block for execution was ready outside one of the gates

DAMON'S RIDE

of Syracuse. Great crowds gathered, for it was known that Damon had not returned and that Pythias must die for his friend.

He was led out of the prison and Dionysius said, "Your friend has not come back to die. You foolishly thought he would keep his promise. I knew better. Do not ask for mercy; none will be granted."

Pythias said, "I ask no mercy. Damon is either sick or dead, for he would never break his word. He would be faithful to me as I am faithful to him."

The sun sank down in the western sky. Pythias was led up the steps of the platform, where the block stood on which he was to be beheaded. The people were sorry, for he was brave and noble, but Dionysius was glad.

Suddenly there was a stir at the edge of the crowd. A shout arose from the same direction. Everybody turned to look. A horse, gray with foam and dust, burst through the ranks of people and Damon leaped from his back.

"Forgive me, Pythias," he cried. "I could not come sooner, but I am yet in time."

One long, loud cry went up from the crowded square.

"Pardon, pardon for Damon," was the shout.

Dionysius bowed his proud head. "Release the prisoner," he ordered. "Let there be three true friends," he said, "Damon and Pythias and myself."

CHAPTER LVIII

THE WISE MAN WHO LISPED

A LITTLE seaport of Greece, called Stageira, was the birthplace of Aristotle. His father was a doctor and attended the king of Macedonia. He took his young son to that court, where the boy became a friend of the prince of Macedonia, who was afterwards known as King Philip.

When Aristotle was seventeen years old his father and mother died, and he went to Athens, that he might attend the school of Plato. That teacher was absent at the time and Aristotle studied without his help. He not only read books but talked with the wisest men of the city.

When Plato came back, he was glad to have this lad as a scholar. He was very proud of him and said, "Aristotle is the mind of my school."

Pointing to the home of the young man, he said, "That is the house of the reader. I am only afraid he will study too much. He needs a curb; others must feel the spur."

They spent twenty years together as teacher and

scholar. For ten years of that time, however, Aristotle was a teacher also and gathered around him a fine company of young men.

When Plato died Aristotle left Athens and went to travel in other lands. Philip, who had become king of Macedonia, sent him a letter in which he said,—

"Friend of my youth, I wrote you long ago that I had a son of whom I hoped great things. He is now thirteen years old and nobody can do anything with him. He is determined always to have his own way. I know that you are wise and gentle and good. Come and teach him to be like yourself."

Aristotle went to Macedonia and took charge of the boy, who later became the famous Alexander the Great. Philip was very glad to see the philosopher, and said, "My friend, what shall I do to please and help you?"

Aristotle answered, "O king, by your orders my native city of Stageira has been destroyed and now lies in ruins. Rebuild that town and let me take the young prince there to study with me."

The king gladly did that and built there, in a pleasant grove, a gymnasium for the teacher and his pupils, Alexander and his young friends.

The prince loved Aristotle and willingly learned his lessons in poetry, eloquence, philosophy, literature, and medicine. He gained many noble thoughts also and was trained to be kind, generous, just, and honorable. They spent four happy years together; and after that

Alexander often took Aristotle's advice and did what his old teacher thought best.

When Alexander became king of Macedonia, Aristotle went back to Athens, where he was welcomed with joy. The government of the city gave him a gymnasium called the Lyceum because it was near the temple of Apollo Lyceios. Like the school at Stageira, it had pleasant, shady walks, called in Greek "peripatoi." Many scholars went there; and Aristotle, instead of sitting down inside the house, liked to walk up and down the paths, lecturing to his pupils. For that reason he and those who thought like him were called "peripatetic philosophers,"—that is, "the wise men who walked about."

In the morning he lectured on deep subjects but in the afternoon he spoke of things easier to understand. Every ten days the scholars elected a new ruler, or archon, who governed them until they chose another. Besides philosophy, they were taught good manners and politeness, for some of them were disposed to be rough and rude at their meals and in social meetings.

Aristotle lived at Athens for thirteen years, busy in writing books when he was not teaching. He was very fond of natural history, and one of his books was upon the *History of Animals*. Alexander gave him a great deal of money and sent him many curiosities for a museum he was gathering.

After Alexander died Greece made war against Macedonia. Because Aristotle had been a friend of Philip and Alexander it was said that he was an enemy of Athens. His enemies wanted to get rid of him, but he was so good and kind, as everybody knew, that it was difficult to find any fault in him. At last this was said:—

"O Athenians, this man Aristotle has insulted the holy gods! His friend Hermias was only a man, as we all knew; yet this fellow has written a hymn praising Hermias as if he were a god. More than that, in honor of him this man has laid upon altars such gifts and sacrifices as ought only to be offered to the immortal gods. Away with this wicked wretch from our city!"

When Aristotle heard that he went away. Some friends urged him to stay and take his trial, but he said,—

"I remember how the men of Athens put Socrates to death. I do not wish to be treated as he was, so I will go away in good time."

After he had gone his trial came on. All his rights and honors were taken away and he was condemned to death.

He did not go back to Athens but died peacefully when he was sixty years old.

His body was carried to Stageira and buried there with honor. A yearly festival was kept sacred to his memory.

He was a short, slight man, never very strong, but lively and agreeable in his manners. He liked to be well dressed and was careful of his clothes. His eyes were small and he spoke with a kind of lisp. Strangers might laugh at that, but his friends never thought of it, for they knew his real greatness and wisdom.

CHAPTER LIX

THE MAN WHO WAS CALLED "THE GOOD"

P HOCION, called the Good, was an aristocrat; that is, he believed that the few who were wise and rich, and nobly born should govern the masses of the people.

While he was a lad he attended Plato's lectures. He was quite young when he was ordered to take twenty vessels and go to collect tribute from the states friendly to Athens. He said, "These are too many for friends and not enough for enemies." At last he was allowed to go with one vessel and to pay all the expenses.

He succeeded so well that many ships sailed back with him carrying the tribute money.

At the battle of Naxos he led the left wing of the army and helped to win a great victory over the Spartans. He also commanded the forces sent by Athens to help Plutarch the tyrant against Philip of Macedonia, but was not welcomed by those whom he went to aid. He won a victory however and went back to Athens.

Philip of Macedonia while attacking Byzantium

wrote a letter saying that the Athenians had broken their promise that they would help him. Demosthenes told the citizens that this was a declaration of war. Phocion led troops to help the Byzantines, and drove away Philip and his army.

Philip then offered to make peace but Demosthenes would not agree. He said, "If we keep on fighting at a distance we shall keep war away from Attica."

Phocion replied, "The question is not where shall we fight but how shall we conquer. Only victory will keep war at a distance. If we are beaten danger will soon be at our gates."

The Athenians lost the battle of Chæronea and then agreed to a general peace. They found that they must supply Philip with ships and horse soldiers.

Phocion said, "I was afraid of this, but now you must keep the treaty. The men of other days who knew how to make laws and to obey laws were the men who saved Greece."

When Philip died Phocion told the citizens that they must not rejoice at the death even of an enemy. Demosthenes advised Athens not to submit to Alexander. Phocion said it would be better to do so but he told Alexander, "If you want peace, stop fighting. If you want glory, let the Greeks alone and make war on the barbarians."

Alexander thought that was good advice. He sent a present which Phocion would not accept. Then he offered him the mastery of any one of four cities but Phocion again said, "No!"

When Alexander was dead Phocion sent to Antipater, the new king of Macedonia, and asked him to be at peace with Athens. Antipater was willing and made Phocion chief ruler of Athens. Many citizens were driven out of the city, and the power of the people (democracy) was for a time entirely broken.

Affairs changed when Antipater died. The exiled Athenians went back to their homes and set up again the democracy. Phocion and all who had held office under him were condemned to banishment or to death.

The chieftain fled but was brought back and was tried in the courts. Those who wished to speak in his favor were hooted down. He was condemned to death and, like Socrates, he drank a cup of hemlock and died.

When he was gone the mob were sorry. They remembered his goodness and wisdom, all the kindness he had shown and all the glory he had gained for Athens. They gave him a public funeral, showing to his memory every honor possible; and built for him a monument of brass.

He was certainly a great soldier for he had been elected general forty-five times. No more honest and just man ever lived in Athens. His one desire had been to serve his country no matter what happened to himself.

Although his heart was kind his looks were

frowning and alarming. Strangers were afraid to speak to him unless they had a friend to plead for them. He was not an orator like Demosthenes but, in opposition to him, the people were often convinced by Phocion. Once he was seen in the theater paying no attention to what was going on. Some one said, "What, Phocion! Wrapped up in your own thoughts?"

"Yes," he answered. "I am trying to shorten what I have to say to the Athenians."

Demosthenes once warned him, "Take care! If you make the people angry they will kill you!"

Phocion answered, "That may be, but if they keep their sober senses they will kill you!"

CHAPTER LX

ALEXANDER THE GREAT

WHEN Philip died, his son Alexander became king of Macedonia. He was only twenty years of age, but he had received an unusual education. When he was a boy he was taught to work hard and to bear suffering. Aristotle taught him the love of discovery and the rules of government. In war his father was his teacher, and there was none better.

He was a strong and daring boy, who loved horses and athletic sports. His father had a magnificent horse which nobody could ride. Philip ordered that the beast should be killed but the prince asked that he might try what he could do with the animal. The horse was large, powerful, fierce, and shining black in color. Either because his head was like that of an ox, or because he had a white spot of that shape on his nose, he was called Bucephalus which means "ox-head."

Alexander had noticed that the horse was afraid of his own shadow. The boy turned the animal's head to the sun and sprang on his back. The horse reared, plunged, struggled, and ran away; but the prince would not be thrown and at last brought Bucephalus galloping back to the place from which he started. From that hour the prince was master and the horse obeyed every word.

When Alexander took the throne he had many enemies. He did not wait for them to act. Those who were near him he put in prison; then marched into the south of Greece and at once took Thebes. Every house, except that of the poet Pindar, was pulled down and the people who were not killed were sold into slavery. The Greek states, except Sparta, held a congress at Corinth and elected Alexander leader of the war against Persia.

The Persian army met him on the east bank of the river Granicus but were soon defeated. Several cities opened their gates to him and he was quickly master of Asia Minor.

In Phrygia he was told of the Gordian knot. A peasant named Gordius had become king. He had tied his wagon and harness together with a very hard knot and had consecrated them to Zeus. It was a common saying that whoever should untie that knot should be master of the world.

Alexander went into the temple; looked at the knot for a moment; then cut it with his sword.

"I have unfastened the knot," he said. "Now let the oracle be fulfilled."

The next year he marched farther east and met the army of Darius near Issus. Alexander as usual gained the victory. Darius fled, but his wife, daughters, and son remained in the conqueror's hands. He treated them with such kindness that Darius afterwards thanked him for his mercy.

The march was now southward through Syria and Palestine. Tyre kept its gates closed against him for seven months. When it was captured many of the citizens were put to death, and thirty thousand were sold as slaves.

Alexander then, it is said, went to Jerusalem, intending to destroy it; but the high priest met him outside the walls and persuaded the young conqueror to do no harm to the ancient city.

He then visited Egypt where he had an easy victory. At the mouth of the west branch of the river Nile he founded the city of Alexandria, that it might be the center of commerce for the eastern and western worlds.

He then moved eastward to Persia to meet again Darius. "The sky cannot hold two suns," he said, "and the world cannot have two masters. Darius must conquer or I will."

Near Arbela the Persian army was camped consisting of more than a million of men with cavalry, chariots with scythes fastened to the wheels, and fifteen elephants. Alexander had less than fifty thousand men but they were all trained warriors. Darius fought well for a time but nothing could stand before the man of Macedonia. Thousands after thousands of the barbarians fell and soon the remnant of their army was in motion flying from the fatal field. Darius escaped, but

ALEXANDER TRAINING BUCEPHALUS

his tents, baggage, and treasures were left and became the property of the Greeks.

Darius without an army, almost without a nation, fled across the mountains to Media. Alexander steadily followed him until at last the poor Persian refused to retreat any farther. The governor of Bactria, Bessus by name, killed him, thinking thus to please the approaching conqueror. But Alexander was both sorry and angry at this base treason and needless murder.

He now changed entirely his way of living. When he first saw the tent of Darius with its elegant and expensive furniture, he said, "This is truly the way for a king to live." After the final defeat of the Persians he grew very extravagant. The dishes upon his table were made of gold and the food was rich and expensive. He drank far too much wine and let his anger rage without control. He thought his friends were turned against him and wanted to take his life. For that reason he had a number of them put to death.

CHAPTER LXI

THE WISE MAN WHO LIVED IN A TUB

A STRANGE character of those old days was called Diogenes. He was not born at Athens but went there a young man and spent his time and money in folly and waste. When everything was gone he looked around to know what he should do.

In the street one day he saw a crowd following a man very poorly dressed who with a stick tried to drive away his followers.

"Who is that and why do the people crowd about him?" asked Diogenes.

He was told, "That is Antisthenes. He was a friend of the great Socrates and was with him when he died. He teaches strange lessons and the crowd like to hear him but he drives them away."

"What does he teach?" Diogenes inquired.

"Oh," was the reply, "he says that pleasure is an evil and a hurt, and that men ought not to love themselves, or their families, or the state, or anything, except to do good."

Diogenes went to Antisthenes, and said, "Let me be your scholar."

"Go away," said the other. "I want no scholars. Socrates had them, and he is dead by poison."

"I want you to teach me how to live," said Diogenes. "I have spent all my money and I have no home."

"Live like a dog," was the answer. "Sleep in the streets, eat what you can pick up, do harm to none, do good wherever you can."

Antisthenes was one of the philosophers called "Cynics," which means "dog-like," because they lived as he told Diogenes to do.

"Very well," said Diogenes. "That way of living suits me. I will do as you say. You are my teacher and no stick is heavy enough to drive me away from you."

He did more than his master. To make himself uncomfortable in the summer he rolled in hot sand; in the winter he sat in heaps of snow. His clothes were very coarse and poor. His food was of the plainest and he often ate raw meat. At night he slept under the porches of houses or in the open streets. At last he found a large, empty tub belonging to a temple, and made that his home. This tub was not of wood but of earthenware, and was really a large jar laid on its side. Some boys broke it for mischief, and the city of Athens bought Diogenes a new one.

Although he seemed very cross and surly he

had a kind heart. Everybody respected him highly and nobody was angry at him for his plain talk. He said, "Nothing is useful unless it does good immediately. Men read about the wrongs of Ulysses but do not try to right their own wrongs. Of what use is their reading?

"Musicians are very particular to have their lyres in tune but their minds are often harsh and jangling. Of what use is music then?

"Astronomers tell us about the moon and stars while their wives and children are ragged and hungry. Orators go about saying what is right but doing wrong. Of what use is all that?"

It is said that once he was seen in broad daylight going through the streets with a lighted lantern in his hand.

"Have you lost something, Diogenes?" he was asked.

"No," he answered, "but I am trying to find an honest man."

Alexander the Great had heard of this strange man, and went to see him. When he saw Diogenes sitting in his tub he said, "I am Alexander the Great."

"Well," said the other, "I am Diogenes the Cynic."

"I should be pleased to do anything for you. What should you like me to do?" asked the king.

"Stand out of my sunshine," was the reply.

"STAND OUT OF MY SUNSHINE!"

Alexander was not angry. He said, "If I were not Alexander I should like to be Diogenes."

For some reason the philosopher went on a voyage to Ægina. The vessel was taken by pirates and he was carried to Crete and sold as a slave.

The merchant who first bought him asked him, "What can you do?"

"I can command men," he answered. "Sell me to somebody who needs a ruler."

A man from Corinth went through the market looking for a slave to buy. He was told about Diogenes. "That is the man I want," he said, and bought him.

When they arrived at Corinth the man said, "I see that you are wise and good. You are now free; but come, live in my house, teach my children, and be my friend."

All this Diogenes did, and we do not hear that he objected to sleeping in a bed or to sitting at a table.

The man with whom he lived said, "He is a good man and the good spirit of my house."

Every winter he went to Athens and spent some time there. He lived to be ninety years old and many friends mourned when he died.

CHAPTER LXII

THE END OF GLORY

AT the battle of the Granicus a man named Clitus had saved Alexander's life. For this he was now to be made governor of a province. The night before he was to start for his new home, the king gave a feast, at which a dispute arose. Clitus said, "Yes; soldiers win the victories, and generals reap the glory." Alexander rushed angrily toward him but Clitus was pushed out of the room. Alexander seized a spear and tried to follow him. Clitus, full of rage, came back and Alexander struck him dead. The once noble young king had become fierce and cruel.

Alexander decided to make his home in the East, and to please the people he married Roxana, a princess of the country.

Babylon and Susa, large, rich and beautiful cities, now belonged to Alexander. But he could not stay long anywhere. He marched to Persepolis, the capital of Persia, and made that his own. There he gave a magnificent feast to his friends and to the nobles of the place. He had brought from Thebes a famous singer named Timotheus, who played on the flute and the lyre and who led a large company of singers. Alexander sat on a splendid throne to show that he was master of the world. Timotheus with his music excited the people so that they called out, "Alexander is more than man! He is a god!" The foolish man pretended to believe them and allowed them to worship him.

Then Timotheus sang about the Greeks who had been killed in battle; and Alexander drunk with wine and rage ordered his men to set fire to the palace in which they were then feasting. He wished to burn the city in revenge for the loss of so many friends who had fallen in the wars.

He stayed four years in Persia conquering every leader who dared oppose him, and giving orders for the government of all the countries of which he was master. He had many faults but some virtues remained with him, and he tried to improve the condition of people. He built cities, one of them named after his horse Bucephalus, which died of wounds received in battle, and for which Alexander sincerely grieved. He established libraries and schools and had the people taught the Greek language. He opened the way into the far East and made it possible for men to travel by land and sea into strange countries.

After the four years he led his army into India to conquer that vast country. There he had a fierce battle with King Porus, who used trained elephants in his army but who was defeated and taken prisoner. Still marching eastward, Alexander reached the river Hyphasis, the most eastern branch of the river Indus.

There his soldiers rebelled. They had been many years from home and were always being led farther away from Greece. They said, "Our fathers and mothers, our wives and children and friends, are in that land. Shall we ever see it again? We are here in a strange world and the word is always 'Forward!' We will not go forward; we will not cross this river."

Alexander could not persuade them to change their minds. He built a fleet of vessels and sent them, filled with soldiers, down the river, while with eight thousand men he marched along the banks fighting and conquering all the way. In one of these fights he was wounded and when they again reached Persia he went to Susa to rest.

Here he induced eighty of his officers and ten thousand of his troops to marry Asiatic women. To all such he gave handsome wedding presents. He also took many Asiatic men into his army and taught them how to march and to fight like the Greeks.

In the spring of 324 B.C. he went to Babylon intending to make that the capital city of the world. The magicians, or wise men, had told him that to go to that place would be fatal to him but he paid no attention to their warning.

His thoughts were gloomy and he was in very low spirits. He had caught malarial fever in the marshes of the Tigris and he injured himself by the use of strong drink. After a short illness all could see that he must soon die.

His friends said to him, "O mighty king, who shall take the kingdom after you are gone?"

He answered, "The strongest." His signet ring he gave to Perdiccas, who was afterwards made commander-in-chief of the army. Alexander was not thirty-three years old when he died and he had reigned less than thirteen years. His life had been full of battle and victory but he could not escape death.

He was buried in Babylon but his body was afterwards removed to Alexandria where it was interred in a coffin of gold.

His Macedonian officers divided his vast empire among them but none of them was great enough to be a true leader, and they quarreled and killed one another. Perdiccas was one of those who were put to death.

CHAPTER LXIII

THE GREAT MECHANIC

S YRACUSE in Sicily was a Greek colony. Nearly three hundred years before the time of Christ a boy was born in that city, who grew up to be a most wonderful man. It is said that he was a relative of the king of Syracuse, who was very fond of him and whom he helped in war against the Romans.

This boy was named Archimedes. He had a deep love for geometry and became a great astronomer according to the learning of his time. He invented many wonderful machines which were used to protect his city in time of war. Some of these threw darts and stones against the enemies who came by land; others cast huge rocks upon the ships that sailed into the harbor to attack the city.

Marcellus, the Roman general, thought that these machines could only throw a long distance and that, as his vessels came nearer, the stones would fly over them and do no harm. But Archimedes had arranged his engines so that when the ships drew near the rocks crashed upon them, breaking their masts, knocking overboard the rowers, and often sinking the vessels.

It is said that he placed rows of burning-glasses so that they set fire to the Roman vessels when they were far off; and that he made a long arm which reached out from the wall, caught one of the enemy's boats and turned it around like a toy.

At any rate he made Marcellus afraid to come near the city, either by land or sea. The soldiers and the vessels stayed out of reach and watched Syracuse so that nobody could go in or come out. This they did for three years hoping to conquer the people by starvation.

Archimedes did much more than protect the city. He had a very busy mind and wrote books, copies of which are in the great libraries of the world to-day. He found out many wonderful truths and set them down in writing and it was nearly two thousand years before men learned more than he had taught about those subjects.

Here is a story often told in regard to him.

The king of Syracuse had given a jeweler a certain weight of gold to be made into a crown. He did not feel satisfied that all the gold had been used for that purpose.

He called Archimedes and said, "Cousin, I think my jeweler has cheated me. The crown weighs as much as the gold I gave him, but I believe he has kept some of it and put silver in its place. You know many things; can you help me find out the truth about this?"

Archimedes said, "I do not know how that can be done but I will try."

He thought a long time but saw no way to answer the question. One day he was taking a bath and noticed for the first time that his body pushed away just so much water. The thought flashed into his mind, "Gold is heavier than silver and takes up less room. It will then push aside less water. I have found the secret." A few minutes later the people of Syracuse were astonished to see him running through the streets to his home crying out, "*Eureka! Eureka!*" which means, "I have found it! I have found it!"

He put the crown into water and noticed how much of the liquid was pushed aside. Then he took the same weight of gold and tried that. The gold pushed away less than the crown. Then he tried silver which displaced more water; and at last he found out exactly how much silver had been mixed with gold in making the crown.

Do you know what a lever is? It is a stick or bar by which men can easily move heavy weights. Archimedes used that tool a great deal and said, "Give me a place on which to stand and I will move the world!" But he never found that place.

He was so busy with his studies that he did not know when the Romans captured Syracuse. After three years of waiting Marcellus entered and took possession of the rich and beautiful city. He did not mean to harm Archimedes, so he sent a soldier to bring the great man to him. The warrior found the student bending over his books and told him that he must go to the general. Archimedes asked him to please wait a little until he had finished his study. The soldier did not know who this gray old man was but he killed him with a blow of his sword.

Marcellus was very sorry. He made a great funeral for Archimedes and built over his grave a monument on which was carved a sphere and cylinder. Archimedes had been greatly pleased with himself for finding out the relation between these two bodies.

One hundred and thirty-six years afterwards the famous Roman, Cicero, went to Syracuse. The chief men of the city said, "What shall we show you first?" He answered, "Lead me to the tomb of Archimedes."

They replied, "We have never seen it. We do not know where it is!"

Cicero went alone, and searched the cemeteries. In one place he found bushes and briers with the top of a pillar showing above them. He cleared away the brambles and there was the grave of Archimedes and above it his monument, engraved with the sphere and cylinder which he had wished should mark his last resting-place.

CHAPTER LXIV

CONQUERED BY ROME

T HE vast empire of Alexander the Great was kept together by Perdiccas for two years. He was only the chief minister who gave advice and orders but was not called king. Alexander's baby son and his half-brother were kings and four under rulers were appointed, two in Europe and two in Asia. Lands were given to ten of the generals to govern in the name of the kings.

After two years great changes took place, and the empire was divided into four kingdoms. War went on nearly all the time and Athens suffered such heavy losses that she had only nine thousand citizens left.

While Greece had been making history a new power had slowly arisen in the world. Rome, at first a little city on the banks of the Tiber in Italy, had conquered the neighboring tribes, and its armies had then marched against other nations, crossing mountains, rivers, and even seas. The Roman soldiers instead of flags carried brass eagles upon poles; and while Alexander was fighting and conquering in the

East those eagles were being moved farther and farther in all directions.

The time at last came when the Greeks and the Romans met and struggled for the mastery. But they did not find a clear stage on which to fight their battles. Other powerful and warlike nations had also come forward during these times. Among these were the Gauls, a barbarous people living in what is now France. They sent out armies which fought with both Romans and Greeks. One of their chiefs, named Brennus, led two hundred thousand men through Thessaly. The people fled to the mountains for refuge and he burned their houses and crops. A Greek army met him at Thermopylæ where Leonidas had kept the pass two hundred years before. This time also the fighting was fierce and, just as in the old times Xerxes gained the victory, so Brennus defeated the Greeks by crossing the mountain and attacking them from the rear.

The savage Brennus then led his soldiers to Delphi expecting to become rich by robbing the temple. Four thousand Greeks met him on Mount Parnassus and held him in check. The sky grew dark with clouds, the wind blew strongly, a heavy snowstorm came on. The Gauls were blinded with the snow and chilled with the cold. Their leader was badly wounded. The army broke up into little companies and wandered among the mountains starving and freezing.

Other tribes of Gauls had entered Italy and were fighting against Rome, which had treated them very cruelly. Their principal stronghold was Tarentum, in the southeastern part of Italy. They asked Pyrrhus, king of Epirus, to come over and help them. He raised an army of twenty-five thousand men and taking with him twenty elephants crossed the Ionian Sea and landed near Tarentum.

In the first battle with the Romans the Greeks were seven times driven from the field and seven times fought their way back to it. When Pyrrhus brought up his elephants the Roman horses ran away, and the Greek king gained a complete victory.

He won many more battles and proved himself to be a great general. But times came when he was beaten and in order to get money to pay his troops he sent a ship to Locri to take the treasures from the temple there. The vessel started back loaded with riches but was wrecked upon the shore. Pyrrhus believed that the goddess was angry with him and he sent the treasure back to the temple. But he never again had success and he thought it was because the curse of the deity followed him. He went home to Greece and never returned to Italy.

Philip V, king of Macedonia, was a young man of great ability. He defeated the enemies who lived near his own land and then attacked a Roman colony on the west coast of Greece. If he conquered there he intended to cross into Italy and carry on the war. He was defeated and could not do as he had intended.

He kept on fighting however. Some of the Greek states took his part; others were on the side of Rome. The Roman general sent out word that all the Greeks should be free and that he would fight for them against Macedonia. This good news brought nearly all the Greek states over to the Roman side, and Macedonia was attacked in every direction, by land and by sea. Philip was beaten in a great battle and was compelled to give up all his Greek cities outside Macedonia, to surrender his entire navy, and to pay a million and a quarter of dollars.

After a few more years of fighting Macedonia and Greece fell completely into the power of Rome. The days of liberty and glory were over. But the Romans studied the Greek philosophy, read the Greek poets, copied the Greek art, and built their magnificent temples and palaces after the Greek manner. They could not excel their conquered subjects; they could only follow them. In that way the glory of Greece continues. While the world stands it will bear the mark made by Athens in the days when she was strong and wise and beautiful.

PRONUNCIATION GUIDE

A

Abydos (a-bī′dos)

Academus (ak-a-dē′mus)

Academy (ak-ad′-em-i)

Achilles (a-kil′ēs)

Acrisius (a-kris′i-us)

Acropolis (a-krop′ō-lis)

Admetus (ad-mē′tus)

Adrastus (a-dras′tus)

Ægean sea (ē-jē′-an se′)

Ægeus (ē-jūs)

Ægina (ē-jī′na)

Æolus (ē-o′lus)

Æschylus (es′ki-lus)

Æsculapius (es-kū-lā′pi-us)

Æthiopians (e-thi-ō′pi-ans)

Ætna (et′na)

Agamemnon (ag-a-mem′non)

Ajax (ā′jaks)

Alcæus (al-sē′us)

Alcestis (al-ses′tis)

Alcibiades (al-si-bī′a-dēz)

Alexander (al-eg-zan′der)

Alexandria (al-eg-zan′dri-a)

Alpheus (al′fē-us)

Amasis (a-mā′sis)

Amazons (am′a-zonz)

Amphitrite (am-fi-trī′te)

Anacreon (a-nak′rē-on)

Andromeda (an drom′e da)

Antiochus (an ti′ō kus)

Antipater (an tip′a ter)

Antisthenes (an tis′the nēz)

Apelles (a pel′ēz)

Aphrodite (af rō dī′te)

Apollo (a pol′o)

Apollo Lyceios
   (a pol′o li cē′yos)

Arbela (ar bē′la)

Arcadia (ar kā′di a)

Archilochus (ar kil′ō kus)

Archimedes (ar ki mē′dēz)

Archon (ar′kon)

Areopagus (ā rē op′a gus)

Ares (ā′rēz)

Arethusa (ar ē thū′sa)

Argo (ar′gō)

Argonauts (ar′go nâtz)

Argos (ar′gos)

Argus (ar′gus)

Ariadne (ar i ad′nē)

Ariæus (a ri ē′us)

Arion (a rī′on)

Aristides (ar is tī′dēz)

Aristocles (a ris′to clēs)

Aristophanes (ar is tof′a nēz)

Aristotle (ar'is tot l)
Armenia (ar mē'ni a)
Artaxerxes (ar taks erks'ēz)
Artemis (ar'tē mis)
Atalanta (at a lan'ta)
Athene (a thē'ne)
Atlas (at'las)
Attica (at'i ka)
Atys (at'is)
Augean (â jē'an)
Aulis (â'lis)

B
Babylon (bab'i lon)
Bacchus (bak'us)
Bactria (bak'tri a)
Bellerophon (be ler'ō fon)
Bessus (bes'us)
Bias (bī'as)
Bœotia (be ō'sh i a)
Brennus (bren'us)
Bucephalus (bū sef'a lus)
Byzantines (bi'zan tines)
Byzantium (bi'zan tium)

C
Cadmus (kad'mus)
Callisto (ka lis'to)
Calypso (ka lip'so)
Cassandra (ka san'dra)
Castalia (kas tā'li a)

Cecropia (se krō'pi a)
Cecrops (sē'krops)
Cephissus (se fis'us)
Cerberus (ser'be rus)
Ceres (sē'rēz)
Chæronea (ker ō nē'a)
Charon (kā'ron)
Charybdis (ka rib'dis)
Chilo (kī'lō)
Chimæra (ki mē'ra)
Chios (kī'os)
Chiron (kī'ron)
Cicero (sis'e rō)
Cimon (si'mon)
Circe (ser'sē)
Clearchus (klē ar'kus)
Cleobulus (klē ō bū'lus)
Clitus (klī'tus)
Colchis (kol'kis)
Conon (kō'non)
Corinna (kō rin'a)
Corinth (kor'inth)
Corinthian (kor in'thi an)
Crete (krēt)
Crœsus (krē'sus)
Crotona (krō tō'na)
Cunaxa (kū naks'a)
Cupid (kū'pid)
Cybele (sib ē'le or sib'e lē)
Cyclopes (si'klō pēz)
Cyclops (sī'klops)

Cyprus (sī'prus)

Cyrus (sī'rus)

D

Dædalus (ded'a lus)

Damon (dā'mon)

Danaë (dan'a e)

Dardanelles (dar da nelz')

Darius (da rī'us)

Delos (dē'los)

Delphi (del'fĭ)

Demaratus (dem a rā'tus)

Demeter (de mē'ter)

Demosthenes
(dē mos'thē nēz)

Deucalion (dū kā'li on)

Diana (dī an'a)

Diogenes (dī oj'e nēz)

Dionysius the Elder
(dī ō nish'i us)

Dionysius the Younger
(dī ō nish'i us)

Dionysus (dī ō nī'sus)

Dis (dis)

Discord (dis'kord)

Dodona (dō dō'na)

Doric (dor'ik)

Doriscus (dō ris'kus)

Draco (drā'kō)

Dryads (drī'ads)

E

Egypt (ē'jipt)

Elis (ē'lis)

Endymion (en dim'i on)

Eos (ē'os)

Epaminondas
(e pam i non'das)

Ephesus (ef'e sus)

Epimetheus (ep i mē'thūs)

Epirus (e pī'rus)

Eros (ē'ros)

Erysichthon (er y sik'thon)

Eureka (ū rē'ka)

Euripides (ū rip'i dēz)

Europa (ū rō'pa)

Eurotas (ū rō'tas)

Eurydice (ū rid'i sē)

Euxine (ūk'sin)

G

Ganymede (gan'i mēd)

Gauls (gâlz)

Geryon (je rī' on)

Golden Fleece (gold'en flēs)

Gordian (gôr'di an)

Gordius (gôr'di us)

Gorgon (gôr'gon)

Granicus (gra nī'kus)

H

Hamadryads
 (ham'a dri'adz)

Hebe (hē'bē)

Hector (hek'tor)

Hecuba (hek'ū ba)

Helen (hel'en)

Helicon (hel'i kon)

Hellas (hel'as)

Helle (hel'ē)

Hellenes (hel lē'nēz)

Hellespont (hel'es pont)

Helots (hē'lots)

Hephæstus (hē fes'tus)

Hera (hē'ra)

Heracles (her'a klēz)

Hercules (her'ku lēz)

Hermes (her'mēz)

Hermias (her mī'as)

Herodotus (he rod'otus)

Hesiod (he'si od)

Hesperides (hes per'i dēz)

Hesperus (hes'per us)

Hestia (hes'ti a)

Hippias (hip'i as)

Hippomenes (hi pom'en ēz)

Homer (hō'mer)

Homeric hymns
 (hō měr'ik hims)

Hyades (hī'a dēz)

Hydra (hī'dra)

Hylas (hī'las)

Hyperboreans
 (hī per bō'rē anz)

Hyphasis (hif'a sis)

I

Icaria (ī kā'ri a)

Icarus (ik'a rus)

Ichor (ī kôr)

Iliad (il'i ad)

Ilion (il'i on) or
 Ilium (il'i um)

Illyrians (il ir'i ans)

Indus (in'dus)

Ionia (ī ō'ni a)

Ionic (i ō'nik)

Iphigenia (if' i jē nī'a)

Iphitus (if'i tus)

Iris (ī'ris)

Issus (is'us)

Ithaca (ith'a ca)

Ixion (iks ī'on)

J

Jason (jā'son)

Jerusalem (je rū'sa lem)

Juno (jū'no)

Jupiter (jū'pi ter)

L

Lacedæmonia
 (las e dē mō'ni a)

Laconia (la kō'ni a)

Lampsacus (lamp'sa kus)

Laocoön (la ok′ō on)

Latmos (lat′mos)

Latona (la tō′na)

Laurium (lâr′i um)

Lebadea (leb a dē′a)

Lemnos (lem′nos)

Leonidas (lē on′i das)

Lesbos (lez′bos)

Leucothea (lū kō the′a)

Leuctra (lūk′tra)

Libyan (lib′i an)

Lindus (lin′dus)

Locri (lō′kri)

Lotus eaters (lō′tus ēt′erz)

Lyceius (li sē′us)

Lyceum (li sē′um)

Lycia (lis′i a)

Lydia (lid′i a)

Lydian (lid′i an)

Lycurgus (lī ker′gus)

Lysander (lī san′der)

M

Macedonia (mas ē dō′ni a)

Mantinea (man ti nē′a)

Marathon (mar′a thon)

Marcellus (mär sel′us)

Mars (märz)

Medea (mē dē′a)

Media (mē′di a)

Medusa (me dū′sa)

Megara (meg′a ra)

Menelaus (men e lā′us)

Mercurius (mer kū′ri us)

Mercury (mer′ku ri)

Merope (mer′ō pē)

Midas (mīdas)

Miletus (mī lē′tus)

Miltiades (mil tī′a dēz)

Minerva (mĭ ner′va)

Minos (mī′nos)

Minotaur (min′o târ)

Mitylene (mit i lē′nē)

Moly (mō′lē)

Momus (mō′mus)

Morpheus (môr′fūs)

Mount Ida (mount ī′da)

Mount Olympus
  (mount ō lim′pus)

Musæus (mu sē′us)

Muses (mū′sez)

Museum (mū sē′um)

N

Naiads (nā′yadz)

Nausicaa (nâ sik′ā a)

Naxos (nak′sos)

Nemea (nē mē′a)

Nemean (nē mē′an)

Nemesis (nem′e sis)

Neptune (nep′tūn)

Nereids (nē′rē idz)

O

Odeon (ō'dē on)
Odysseus (ō dis'ūs)
Odyssey (od'i si)
Olympia (ō lim'pi a)
Olympiad (ō lim'pi ad)
Olympian (ō lim'pi an)
Olympic (ō lim'pik)
Oreads (ō're adz)
Orion (ō rī'on)
Orœtes (o re'tēz)
Orpheus (or'fē us)
Ostracism (os'tra sism)
Ostracon (os'tra kon)

P

Pactolus (pak tō'lus)
Palæmon (pa lē'mon)
Palestine (pal'es tīn)
Palladium (pal'ā di um)
Pan (pan)
Pancratium
　(pan krā'shi um)
Pandora (pan dō'ra)
Paris (păr'is)
Parnassus (par nas'us)
Paros (pā'ros)
Parrhasius (pa rā'shi us)
Parthenon (pär'the non)
Patroclus (pa trō'klus)
Pegasus (peg'a sus)
Pelasgians (pē las'gi ans)

Peleus (pē'lē us) or (pē'lūs)
Pelias (pē'li as)
Pelopidas (pe lop'i das)
Penelope (pē nel'ō pe)
Pentathlon (pen tath'lon)
Penthesilea (pen'the si lē'a)
Perdiccas (per dik'as)
Periander (per i an'der)
Pericles (per'i klēz)
Peripatetics (per'i pā tet'iks)
Peripatoi (per i pat'oi)
Persephone (per sef'ō nē)
Persepolis (per sep'ō lis)
Perseus (per'sūs)
Phaeton (fā'e ton)
Phaon (fā'on)
Phidias (fid'i as)
Philip (fil'ip)
Philippi (fi lip'ī)
Phintias (fin'ti as)
Phocians (fō'se ans)
Phocion (fō'shĭ on)
Phœbus (fē'bus)
Phœnicia (fe nish' a)
Phrygia (frij'i a)
Pindar (pin'där)
Piræus (pī rē'us)
Pisidians (pi sid'i ans)
Pisistratus (pi sis'tra tus)
Pittacus (pit'a kus)
Platæa (pla tē'a)
Plato (plā'to)

Pleiades (plē'ya dēz)
Plutarch (plu'tark)
Pluto (plū'to)
Plutus (plū'tus)
Pnyx (niks)
Polias (po'li as)
Polycrates (po lik'ra tēz)
Polydectes (pol i dek'tēz)
Polyphemus (pol i fē'mus)
Polyxena (po lik'se na)
Porus (pō'rus)
Poseidon (pō sī'don)
Priam (prī'am)
Procrustes (pro krus'tēz)
Prometheus (prō mē'the us
    or prō mē'thūs)
Proserpina (prō ser'pi na)
Proteus (prō'te us)
Pyrrha (pir'ä)
Pyrrhus (pir'us)
Pythagoras (pi thag'ō ras)
Pythias (pith'i as)
Pythoness (pī'thon es)

R

Rhodes (rōdz)
Rhodians (rō'di anz)
Rhœcus (rē'kus)
Romans (rō'mans)
Rome (rōm)
Roxana (roks an'a)

S

Salamis (sal'a mis)
Samos (sā'mos)
Sappho (saf'ō)
Sardis (sar'dis)
Satyrs (sā'ters)
Scheria (skē'ri a)
Scio (sī'ō)
Scylla (sil'a)
Scythia (sith'i a)
Selene (se lē'ne)
Semele (sem'e lē)
Seriphos (se rī'fos)
Sicily (sis'i li)
Silenus (si lē'nus)
Simonides (sī mon'i dēz)
Sinon (sī'non)
Sirens (sī'renz)
Sirius (sir'i us)
Sisyphus (sis'i fus)
Socrates (sok'ra tēz)
Solon (sō'lon)
Sophocles (sof'ō klēz)
Sparta (spär'tä)
Spartans (spar'tans)
Stageira (sta gī'ra)
Stoics (stō'iks)
Styx (sticks)
Susa (sū'sa)
Syracuse (sir'a kūs)
Syria (sir'i a)

T

Tantalus (tan'ta lus)
Tarentum (ta ren'tum)
Tauris (tâ'ris)
Telemachus (te lem'a kus)
Tellus (tel'us)
Terpander (ter pan'der)
Thales (thā'lēz)
Thasos (thā'sos)
Thebans (thē'banz)
Thebes (thēbz)
Themistocles
   (the mis'tō klēz)
Theocritus (thē ok'ri tus)
Thermopylæ (ther mop'i lē)
Theseus (thē'sūs)
Thespians (thes'pi anz)
Thespis (thes'pis)
Thessaly (thes'a li)
Thetis (thē'tis)
Thrace (thrās)
Thucydides (thū sid'i dēz)
Tiber (tī'bur)
Tigris (tī'gris)
Timandra (tim an'dra)
Timotheus (ti mō'thē us)
Tissaphernes (tis a fer'nēz)
Titans (tī'tanz)
Trebizond (treb'i zond)
Triton (trī'ton)
Trojans (trō'janz)

Trophonius (trō fō'ni us)
Troy (troi)
Tyre (tīr)

U

Ulysses (ū lis'ēz)

V

Venus (vē'nus)
Vesta (ves'ta)
Vestal (ves'tal)
Vulcan (vul'kan)

X

Xanthippe (zan thip'ē)
Xenophon (zen'ō fon)
Xerxes (zerk'sēz)

Z

Zeus (zūs)
Zeuxis (zūk'sis)